TH   GY

Large Print Rea
Read,
The Fairacre Festival

THE FAIRACRE FESTIVAL & TIGGY

Miss Read

Chivers Press · Thorndike Press
Bath, England   Thorndike, Maine USA

This Large Print edition is published by Chivers Press, England, and by Thorndike Press, USA.

Published in 2000 in the U.K. by arrangement with Penguin.

The Fairacre Festival published in 2000 in the U.S. by arrangement with Houghton Mifflin Company.

Tiggy published in 2000 in the U.S. by arrangement with Penguin Books Limited.

U.K. Hardcover ISBN 0–7540–3996–X (Chivers Large Print)
U.K. Softcover ISBN 0–7540–3997–8 (Camden Large Print)
U.S. Softcover ISBN 0–7862–2314–6 (General Series Edition)

The text of this Large Print edition is unabridged.
Other aspects of the book may vary from the original edition.

Set in 16 pt. New Times Roman.

Printed in Great Britain on acid-free paper.

British Library Cataloguing in Publication Data available

Library of Congress Cataloging-in-Publication Data

Read, Miss.
    The Fairacre Festival / by "Miss Read".
    Tiggy / by "Miss Read".
      p.   cm.
    Titles from separate title pages.
    Originally published: London : M. Joseph, 1968 (1st work), 1971 (2nd work).
    ISBN 0–7862–2314–6 (lg. print : sc : alk. paper)
    1. Fairacre (England : Imaginary place)—Fiction. 2. Country life—England—Fiction. 3. Villages—England—Fiction. 4. Pastoral fiction, English. 5. Large type books. I. Read, Miss. Fairacre Festival. II. Title: Fairacre Festival. III. Title.
PR6069.A42 T54   2000
823'.914—dc21   99–055515

CONTENTS

THE FAIRACRE FESTIVAL

For Anne, with love from her godmother

CHAPTER ONE

On the first night of October a mighty wind arose and smote the countryside around Fairacre. The violence of that wild night took almost all by surprise. Only the exceptionally weatherwise, such as Mr Willet, had any inkling of the devastation which lay in store, and even they admitted, as they surveyed the wreckage the next morning, that it was 'a durn sight worse'n they'd thought it would be'.

We had enjoyed a week of mellow sunshine at the end of September. Butterflies clung decoratively to the Michaelmas daisies, wasps lurched drunkenly from ripe pears to ripe plums, and the schoolchildren at Fairacre School were more comfortable in their cotton frocks and thin shirts than they had been on many other occasions during a changeable summer.

Harvest Festival was celebrated on the last day of September and, as usual, we helped to deck the ancient church of St Patrick's with 'all things bright and beautiful'. Coral-berried bryony from the school hedge wreathed the font. At the foot lay mounds of apples, pears and marrows. Carrots, parsnips and onions lined the ledges, and two fine sheaves of corn gleamed and rustled in their time-honoured place, one on each side of the chancel steps.

The ladies of the parish had put their natural talents, and the expertise learnt at the local floral society, into the handsome flower arrangements, and it was generally maintained by the congregation that the church had never looked so magnificent.

Monday morning dawned as benignly as ever. I watched the children, summer-clad and relaxed, as they drank their morning milk, and congratulated myself on postponing the lighting of the two tortoise stoves. Far too often, in the autumn term, I have asked my curmudgeonly school cleaner, Mrs Pringle, to light these monsters, only to experience a spell of humid weather in which we have all sweltered in the classrooms. Mrs Pringle never lets me forget these unfortunate errors.

'Remember last year?' she demands belligerently, massive jaw out-thrust. 'You would have it. Said the children was cold, and up I come with paper, with sticks, with matches, although my leg was not what it should be—'

'But it *was* cold,' I begin, but am swept aside.

'I fetches the coal, fetches the coke, goes down on me hands and knees for a full quarter of an hour to get the stoves to draw—and what happens?'

I don't bother to answer. This, I know from experience, is a rhetorical question. Sometimes I think what a wonderful actress the stage has lost in Mrs Pringle. Her looks are definitely a drawback, but she has a fine sense of drama and puts plenty of punch into her lines.

'We gets a hot spell. All my work's for nothing, and the coke's got to come out of us ratepayers' pockets. What's more, the children's pores are left hanging open for all the germs to get in as soon as they goes out into the cold playground!'

This year, I told myself, on that fair Monday morning, I had behaved in an exemplary manner. Tomorrow would be October the second, and after that the lighting of the stoves must surely be considered acceptable by my task mistress.

But, by midday, I was beginning to have doubts. The sun went in, the temperature dropped sharply, and the children began to rub their goose-pimpled arms. By the time they ran home in the afternoon, a cold wind had sprung up, snatching the yellow leaves from the plum tree in my garden and sending me scuttling to light my sitting-room fire.

As darkness fell, the force of the wind increased. It roared in the elm trees towering above the school. It screamed round the school house, spattering leaves against the window and sending the dustbin lid clanging across the garden. The little house shuddered at its onslaught. Safe by the leaping fire, with a pile of exercise books to mark and the cat

3

asleep by my feet, I gave the elements scant attention.

But later, in bed, I became anxious. Never before had I heard the wind quite so violent in Fairacre. I remembered the doleful tales about elm trees which Mr Willet never tired of telling me. If one of those hefty branches fell across my roof it could be pretty damaging. And what about the roof tiles? It seemed incredible that anything could withstand the fury of the wind tonight. Strange creaks and groans seemed to come from the loft above me and an ill-fitting window let in a piercing draught accompanied by an ear-splitting whistle.

I pulled the bedclothes up round my ears, thanked heaven that I was a schoolteacher and not a sailor, and slept amidst the uproar.

*   *   *

Throughout the night the wind wreaked destruction. In the streets of Caxley it wrenched slates from roofs and toppled a dozen chimney-pots into the gutters. A flying tile broke the plate-glass window of Howard's restaurant in the market square, and a poor unfortunate man, cycling head down against the onslaught on his way to night shift, was blown from the towpath into the cold waters of the Cax, and there drowned.

Just outside Caxley station a telegraph pole fell across the line throwing all into confusion, and on the road to Beech Green a tree had crashed, tearing down the telephone wires in its fall. But Caxley, tucked in its hollow, came off comparatively lightly. It was the windswept villages on the downs which bore the full brunt of the wind's savagery and it was Fairacre which suffered the most shattering blow.

On a little knoll of high ground between the vicarage and St Patrick's a cluster of ancient elms stands, cradling a rookery in the topmost boughs. We, in Fairacre, admire the way that these lovely old trees form a background to the church. Rosy-purple in spring as the buds swell, providing dense shade in full summer, turning to clear gold in the autumn and spreading a black lacy tracery against the winter skies, they are a constant pleasure to the eye.

But Mr Willet has never been one of their admirers.

'One of these days,' he has said, on many occasions, 'them dratted elms is going to cause trouble. Got no proper root growth, has elms. All spread out too near the surface for my liking. A good wind up top and over they goes.' And he was to be proved right.

About two o'clock the fury of the wind was at its height. Its screaming woke me. The loose window shuddered and thudded, and the roaring outside was terrifying. It must have been this particular gust which caught the tallest of the elms nearest the church and sent it toppling. The topmost branches swept St Patrick's stubby spire, and bent the proud weathercock until it drooped head-down from its twisted stay. The heavy branches came to rest across the nave, scattering tiles and damaging the roof for which the church is famed. The massive trunk lay athwart the graveyard and the old roots, torn from the turf, writhed above a huge gaping hole.

I did not hear the crash; nor do I think anyone else did. The noise was so continuous that it was impossible to pick out any particular incident. But the vicar said later that he awoke at that time and was conscious of some extraordinary commotion at the heart of the storm, and confessed frankly that he had felt frightened.

When light returned, the damage was discovered, and in no time at all a bevy of villagers came to survey the wreckage. Mr Willet was first on the scene, and with commendable magnanimity forebore to say: 'I told you so!' It was he who broke the news to Mr Partridge, the vicar, who was shaving when the bell of the back door rang.

'Bad news, sir,' Mr Willet shouted up to the frothy face which appeared at the bathroom window.

'The greenhouse?' queried the vicar, holding the window against the wind.

'No, sir. The church. Tree across it, sir.'

'Oh, my dear Willet!' cried the vicar, his

6

face puckering in distress. 'What a terrible thing! I will be with you directly.'

The window slammed, and within five minutes the vicar and his wife joined Mr Willet at the scene of the disaster. Several workmen, on their way to their labours, had propped their bicycles against the flint churchyard wall, and stood shaking their heads at the confusion.

'We must get help from Caxley,' said Mrs Partridge decisively. 'There's no one in Fairacre with the equipment to shift that enormous thing.'

'We must indeed, my dear,' agreed the vicar distractedly. There were tears in his blue eyes as he paced from one position to another assessing the appalling damage to his beloved St Patrick's. 'I suppose a crane or some such piece of machinery will be necessary, Willet? I can't bear to think of the wreckage we shall discover when the tree is lifted. I must go inside at once and make sure that everything is safe.'

'I'll come inside with you,' said Mr Willet. 'You wants to watch out that none of them timbers is busted.'

They entered the church while more villagers arrived to inspect the night's work. Here was drama in plenty! The schoolchildren were pleasurably excited by it all, and to a certain extent so were their elders, but there was in addition a shocked solemnity in the face of this tragedy, and thin-lipped Mrs Fowler from Tyler's Row put into words the unspoken thoughts of all when she asked of the villagers at large:

'And who's going to pay for this lot, may I ask?'

It was a question which was to perplex Fairacre for many a long month.

*   *   *

Meanwhile, the work of clearing up the mess began. It was impossible to telephone to Caxley as the Post Office men were busy all the morning repairing the line at Beech Green, but Mr Mawne, churchwarden and member of the Parochial Church Council, set off for Caxley at the vicar's behest.

Henry Mawne is a comparative newcomer to Fairacre, a retired schoolmaster and a keen ornithologist. He and his wife take their fair share of responsibilities in village matters and the vicar, in particular, relishes the friendship and support of this quiet man. His competent handling of church accounts is a source of great comfort to the vicar whose grasp of financial details is hopelessly vague. Mrs Partridge confided once to me that her devout and erudite husband is under the impression that ten pennies make a shilling, and that this fundamental misapprehension is at the root of his difficulties. Certainly parochial affairs have been much more businesslike under Henry

Mawne's administration.

As Mr Mawne expected, the plant hire firm had most of its equipment spread about the country that morning, but a crane was promised for the afternoon and two men set off at once from Caxley to start cutting away branches and to clear the site for the rescue operation. He returned to find the vicar in conversation with his Bishop at the county town, the telephone lines in that direction having miraculously escaped damage. He had already been in touch with the Rural Dean, he told Henry Mawne, when he replaced the receiver, and the diocesan architect would be along as soon as possible to look at the damage.

'But the best news of all, my dear Henry,' cried the vicar, 'is from Jock Graham, who arrived just after you had gone, to say that he will act as our architect without any payment. Isn't that a magnificent gesture?'

'It is indeed,' agreed Mr Mawne. He did not care for this elderly Scot, recently retired, but realized how much this generous offer would mean to the parish.

'You see,' went on the vicar, 'I gather that all the expenses will have to be found by Fairacre. The diocesan people have just made it clear that there can be no money forthcoming from them. It's a parish responsibility. I suppose we must expect a bill of a hundred pounds or so?'

'I should prefer to wait until the diocesan architect has had his look,' said Mr Mawne cautiously, 'but from what I saw this morning, I should say we'd be lucky to get away with anything less than two thousand.'

'*Two thousand?*' quavered the vicar. Horror and stupefaction showed in his face. 'It's impossible, Henry!'

Henry Mawne rose from his seat and patted the vicar's shoulder kindly.

'Cheer up, Gerald,' he said. 'I'm probably hopelessly wrong, but I don't want you to get a shock later on. I think you'll find the bill is going to be a great deal more than a few hundred pounds, that's all.'

But we can't pay it,' protested the vicar helplessly. 'Fairacre can't possibly raise anything more than a hundred at the outside!'

'I'm aware of that,' said his friend.

'And even that amount,' went on the vicar despairingly, 'means a succession of whist drives, fêtes, jumble sales, coffee mornings and all those terrible, terrible affairs. You realize that, Henry?'

'Only too well, Gerald,' replied Henry Mawne, doing his best to suppress a shudder.

The vicar rose from his chair and began to pace distractedly round his desk, his hands clasped behind his back and his brow furrowed. Mr Mawne watched him sympathetically from the doorway. It seemed hard to leave his stricken friend in his present

10

distress, but there was much to be done.

Gerald Partridge stopped suddenly and faced him.

'It is a challenge, Henry! This is something sent by Providence to test us, to strengthen our faith. We must, and shall, restore St Patrick's!'

'That's the way to take it,' agreed Mr Mawne, touched by this brave display of resolution. Closing the study door gently behind him, he returned home through the wind.

*   *   *

When school dinner was over, I made my way to the church to see the extent of the damage. The men were busy clearing the worst of the mess from the churchyard, and I went inside by the west door.

Several people had volunteered to tidy up. Mr and Mrs Willet were there, the two sisters, Margaret and Mary Waters, and various other women.

'Got my washing on the line and come straight up,' said one.

'Had to find my poor hens first,' said another. 'The hen house blew clean off their backs, and they was everywhere from the fir tree to the coal-hole.'

Tales of the night's wrecking flew back and forth as they plied brooms and dustpans.

'The top half of Mr Roberts's hay stack

11

went whirling by our roof.'

'Our Nelly lost three tea towels off the line. And the cat! He *would* go out and it's her belief he's been blown out of the parish.'

Somehow, I suspected, listening to these exchanges, the damages grew at each recital. We enjoy a bit of excitement in Fairacre, and the drama of this wild night would certainly go down, suitably embellished, in local history.

There was a great deal of plaster on the floor of the nave, and the pews were white with dust. Mr Willet was collecting the rubble in a wheelbarrow in the aisle. A dark patch gaped above, in the beautiful hammer-beam roof, but no daylight showed through. Hopes were running high that the damage was only superficial, but more would be known when the surveyor had inspected it.

The pulpit was badly scratched and one of the chandeliers had bounced from its hook, at the time of impact, and lay shattered on the floor.

'No loss!' remarked Mrs Mawne to me in an aside audible to all. 'Hideous Victoriana! Pity the rest didn't come down too!'

Afternoon school was a somewhat distracted affair. The children are always excitable in windy weather, and this fascinating disaster added to their general fidgetiness. Hoping to channel their feelings into some positive and useful work—as exhorted to do by all good educationists—I set them to write an

12

essay on the night's storm.

'And you can illustrate it too,' I added, hoping for a prolonged period of peace in the classroom.

'With crayons?'

'Yes, with crayons.'

Won't be much good. 'Twas all dark. Shan't want no colours.

'Then you can simply use your lead pencil,' I retorted loftily. Disgruntled muttering from the malcontent's desk I ignored pointedly.

An unusual quietness fell upon the room, broken only by laboured breathing as the pangs of composition gripped them, and the stutter of crayons depicting rain. I wandered to the window and gazed out. A drift of dead leaves rustled against the foot of the school wall, and a mat of ivy flapped loosely above it, wrenched from its anchorage by the gale.

The vicarage garden seemed bare of leaves, and through the gaps in the denuded shrubbery I could see several of the helpers making their way home. This, I told myself, certainly brings people together—nothing like a common foe to unite a community.

At that moment, young Tom in the front row raised his hand. His parents are fiercely evangelical, and he is uncomfortably well behaved and a trifle smug.

'How do you spell "Wrath-of-God"?' he inquired earnestly.

'How do you intend to use the phrase?' I

13

asked guardedly.

He turned his attention to the paper before him and read slowly.

' "Our chapel was not hit in the night, but the church was. My mum said it was—" ' He paused and looked up hopefully.

I spelt out the desired phrase. My sympathy went out to those working for Christian unity, and I made a mental note to have a lesson on 'loving thy neighbour as thyself', before the end of the week.

It looked as though Fairacre might profit from it.

CHAPTER TWO

Before Monday came round again, much had happened in the village.

In the first place, Fairacre had put itself to rights as best it could. Broken branches were sawn up into neat logs and stacked inside wood-sheds. Shrubs and standard roses were lashed to new stakes. Slates and tiles were hung again, thatch patched and hen-house roofs replaced and weighted with sizeable flint stones, in case of future gales.

Nelly Potter's cat returned, none the worse for a night out. Mr Roberts, the farmer, retrieved some of his scattered hay, and Mrs Pringle, discovering a child's apron blowing on the hedge, recognized it as one of little Vanessa Emery's and returned it graciously to the child's scatter-brained mother.

'Nearly tore to shreds it was by the time the wind had done with it,' said Mrs Pringle to me, before school one morning, 'but I don't suppose it'll ever see needle and thread in that house. Proper muddler that woman is! Half-past nine when I called in, and she still in her dressing-gown!' Mrs Pringle drew an outraged breath at the very thought, and picked up a cinder which was marring the glossy jet of the stove's surround.

'Still, I will say,' she conceded, as she straightened up with an ominous creaking of whalebone stays, 'that she give me a very nice smile and thanked me for my trouble.'

'Good,' I said absently, rummaging in my drawer for a paperclip.

'*Which*,' boomed Mrs Pringle pointedly, 'is a lot more than some people do!'

And with a pronounced limp she made her way to the lobby.

*   *   *

Mr Willet had cleared up the mess in the school playground, and had continued the good work, in his capacity of church sexton, in the graveyard next door. Luckily, the ancient headstones had escaped injury, for the tree which caused most of the trouble had lodged

15

against the roof of the church, and had been lifted clear by the crane without much difficulty.

The damage to the fabric of the church was Fairacre's most serious problem. Providentially, it was less than had been feared at first. The stout ancient roof beams had stood the blow well, and only three or four would need to be replaced. But much retiling needed to be done to the spire and the nave, and the belfry wanted a stonemason's attention.

'And can you give us any idea of the expense?' asked the vicar anxiously as he, Mr Mawne and Jock Graham accompanied the diocesan architect and his young assistant on the tour of inspection.

The architect peered over his half-glasses and looked solemn.

'Mr Graham will go into figures of course, but I should say, at a rough estimate—'

'A *very* rough estimate,' chimed in the assistant, speaking as one who has often been caught out and hoped to miss the unpleasant experience this time.

'As a *very rough* estimate,' agreed the architect, looking coldly at his colleague, 'somewhere in the region—'

'Only *in the region*,' interjected the assistant sternly.

'Of about one thousand eight hundred pounds to two thousand.'

'*About*, of course, *just about*,' echoed his companion. 'One can never be sure what one will find once the work is in hand, as I am sure Mr Graham will agree. One doesn't want to be too hasty in suggesting a figure.'

'So I noticed,' observed Mr Mawne drily.

His face wore a small satisfied smile. This was the sum he had suggested in the first place to his friend, the vicar, and it was some comfort in this bleak hour to know that he was not far out in his estimation.

The vicar's rosy face, however, showed no sign of pleasure, simply stupefaction and distress. He was quite beyond speech.

'We'll go back and report our findings,' said the architect kindly, tucking his half-glasses into a splendid gold-tooled case. 'And, if Mr Graham wishes, I'll send you the names of some reputable contractors who specialize in church repairs who will, of course, give you a detailed estimate when they have had a look at your little bit of trouble here.'

The vicar opened his mouth as though stung into speech, thought better of it, and said nothing. They crossed the churchyard to the black Humber at the gate.

'I shouldn't worry too much, my dear sir,' said the architect with misplaced heartiness. 'Could have been much worse, you know. Think of Coventry Cathedral. Now there *was* some damage!'

The car drove off, watched by Mr Mawne,

Mr Graham and their stricken friend. As it rounded the bend to the village street, the vicar found his voice.

'I don't like to seem uncharitable, but I hope that I may never see that man again! "Our little bit of trouble" indeed!'

'Take no heed of his havering,' rumbled Jock Graham.

The vicar's lips quivered suddenly.

'But what are we to do? What are we to do?'

Henry Mawne rose to the occasion.

'We will call an emergency meeting of the Parochial Church Council and put on our thinking caps,' he replied firmly. Together they shepherded Gerald Partridge to the haven of his vicarage, and a much-needed cup of coffee.

*   *   *

The Parochial Church Council, all twelve of us, turned up in full force on Friday evening. We met in the vicarage dining-room which was still faintly redolent of the curried lamb and baked apples on which Mr and Mrs Partridge had recently dined.

There were present the vicar, in the chair, Mr Mawne and his wife, Mr Roberts, the other churchwarden and our local farmer, Mr Graham as honorary architect, Mr Willet and myself, all from the village. Mr Basil Bradley and Major Gunning represented

18

Springbourne, which is also in the living of Fairacre's vicar, along with three rather prosperous younger men, who commute daily to the City, thus making up our full complement.

Basil Bradley produces a novel each year and is much thought of in the district. He is called upon to open bazaars and fêtes, and is much in demand as a speaker at various functions, twice rising to the dizzy heights of chief speaker at local Women's Institute group meetings. Since the death of his formidable mother, who guarded his goings-out and comings-in zealously, he has lived alone in a pretty cottage enjoying his freedom. He is a remarkably handsome man, with the ashen fair hair which slips imperceptibly over the years into silver, and the gentle manners born of many years of willing servitude to his tyrant. Men dislike him. Women dote on him, and do their best to get him married. Somehow, I do not think that they will ever be successful.

Major Gunning is as martial as his name, and has a garden full of well-disciplined plants as upright as himself. His paths are straight. His standard roses line them like a guard of honour. A row of poplars stands sentinel upon his skyline. No daisies spangle Major Gunning's lawns, no groundsel mars the beds. And should any pink or poppy droop its pretty head out of its appointed place, then summary execution must be expected.

It was he who spoke first after the vicar had explained the dilemma.

'Open an Appeal Fund. Stick up a good bold board outside the church, and send notices to every man-jack in the parish.'

'Humph!' snorted Mrs Mawne beside him. 'That won't bring in much!'

'And have you any suggestions?' asked Major Gunning, bristling.

'Plenty,' snapped Mrs Mawne, slapping her gloves down on the table challengingly. 'First of all—'

'Address the chair,' put in Mr Mawne.

His wife twitched round exasperatedly and faced the vicar.

'Mr Chairman, I think determined and regular money-raising efforts should be started at once. A weekly whist drive, a weekly dance, a weekly raffle, a weekly coffee morning—'

'But, my dear Mrs Mawne,' pleaded the vicar, 'where is the money to come from?'

'I'm telling you. From all these activities!'

Basil Bradley took upon himself the thankless task of explanation.

'But where, I think our Chairman means, will *the people* get the money? Their wages will remain at the same level. They can't afford to go to so many weekly functions.'

'Thank you,' said the vicar simply. 'That is the position exactly. We must try to think of attracting outside help. The parish itself has no riches.'

20

A gloomy silence fell while we all pondered this sad fact.

'D'you mean that there is no help at all from some body or other?' demanded Mr Roberts at length. 'You know—Ecclesiastical Commissioners or the Diocese, or Friends of Friendless Churches? Something o' that?'

'St Patrick's isn't a *friendless* church,' said the vicar defensively. 'It's a very much-loved church.'

'Yes, indeed. Yes, indeed,' agreed Mr Willet warmly.

'But I'm afraid we have only ourselves to rely on,' went on the vicar. 'The Bishop was deeply sympathetic, but made it quite plain that the parish is solely responsible for these repairs.'

'I think Mrs Mawne's suggestions are on the right lines,' I volunteered. 'If all the village organizations make a particular effort it means that we shall raise quite a decent part of the whole by our own exertions.'

'We could map out a programme,' said Mr Roberts. 'What about a traction engine rally in my big meadow?'

'And a folk-dancing display by the village school?' said Mrs Mawne. I could have made a tart retort, but forbore.

'And a bumper Fur and Feather Whist Drive this autumn?' said Mr Willet.

'I should be very pleased to open my garden next summer,' offered Basil Bradley. 'And

21

provide tea. I've just mastered Chelsea buns.'

'How very clever!' cried Mrs Mawne turning towards him. 'Now they are things which I simply *cannot* manage. Cream horns, almond slices, Victoria sandwiches, gingerbread—I flatter myself I can cope with anything like that, but yeast cookery is my Waterloo. How much sugar do you put in with your yeast?'

The chairman, seeing his meeting dissolve, as is so often the case in village affairs, banged loudly on the table.

'Please, please, ladies and gentlemen! Miss Read and Mrs Mawne have both made the suggestion that we see how much can be raised by superhuman efforts in the village by traditional methods. Can anyone add to this idea?'

A rumbling noise from under Mr Willet's tobacco stained moustache gave warning of wise words to follow. Little did we think, as we waited, that we were witnessing the birth of a momentous brainchild.

'What's wrong with having all these things— or most of 'em, say—in one week next summer? A Festival, like. We hears a lot about the Edinburgh Festival and all their goings-on up there. And there's that chap, Britten, at the Aldwych—'

'Aldeburgh,' put in Basil Bradley.

'Same thing,' said Mr Willet airily. 'He has a Festival by the seaside. Mr Annett's been. He said 'twas a real slap-up affair. Well, what I'm getting at is this. Why can't we have a Fairacre Festival?'

We all gazed at Mr Willet with respect.

'It's a wonderful idea, Willet,' said the vicar. 'Quite wonderful! But do you think people would come?'

'Why not?' demanded Mrs Mawne. 'If they go to Edinburgh, to that perishing cold climate, not to mention the reeking smoke which they admit themselves, then why on earth shouldn't they come here?'

'Perhaps not quite in the same numbers,' said Basil Bradley. 'After all Edinburgh has wonderful concerts and ballets and what-have-you—but I'm sure we could have a Fairacre Festival which would be successful on a more modest scale.'

'Dam' good idea,' announced Mr Roberts. 'One great glorious burst of fête, jumble-sale, concert, whist-drive, bingo, dancing and everything else. If we advertise it well, the money will come rolling in.'

'We might have *Son et Lumière*,' said Major Gunning, 'with St Patrick's as the background. Tell the parish story, you know.'

'Not all of it,' said Mr Willet cautiously. 'There's some things best kept quiet. Take that affair of Ted Grimble's grand-dad now—'

'Yes, well—' the vicar broke in hastily. 'Perhaps we are getting away from the point. Could we have a show of hands for Mr Willet's excellent proposal?'

23

We were all agreed. It was decided to meet again to plan not only the Fairacre Festival for next summer, but also to arrange other money-making efforts, starting immediately.

It was while we were congratulating ourselves, and Mr Willet in particular, on our cleverness, that Henry Mawne spoke up.

'Before we go, I think we should be realistic about these ideas. They will raise a few hundred, I feel sure, and we might raise a few more by donations. But I don't think we can hope to raise even half by these methods.'

'But what else can we do?' pleaded the vicar.

Mr Mawne screwed his propelling pencil slowly, making the lead emerge further and further. He studied it intently as he spoke.

'You said earlier that the parish had no riches. It's not quite true. I hardly like to suggest this but I'm going to. We have, as you all know, locked in the bank and used only at the great church festivals, a valuable old chalice of solid silver and impeccable workmanship. One recently fetched over two thousand pounds. It was not as fine as ours.'

We gazed at Henry Mawne in silence. We were all, I think, a little shocked by his suggestion. To tell the truth, I had not realized the value of the chalice, and had certainly forgotten its existence whilst we had been debating ways and means. The vicar looked horrified and Mrs Mawne surveyed her husband with as much disgust as she would have displayed had he suggested slaughtering her dachshund for lunch.

'Impossible!' she exclaimed.

'Unthinkable!' cried Major Gunning.

'That's not ours to give away,' observed Mr Willet austerely. ' 'Twas given to the church to celebrate Queen Anne's reign. Some relation of old Miss Parr's, so they told us at school, gave it over two hundred and fifty years ago. It belongs to the parish.'

The vicar found his voice.

'Willet is quite right, Henry. The chalice is beyond price, and is in any case only ours on trust. It belongs to St Patrick's.'

'So did its roof,' said Henry Mawne. 'I know the idea is distasteful, but there you are. Is it right to keep such a valuable object locked away, while rain comes through the roof and the church deteriorates? St Patrick's also belongs to the parish. Which is of more use?'

Surprisingly, it was Basil Bradley who came to Henry Mawne's support.

'It has been done before. My uncle's church in Cumberland sold a most beautiful silver paten some years ago. It went to a new church somewhere in Massachusetts where it is very much prized, I can assure you.'

'I daresay,' replied the vicar, a shade frostily. 'But I cannot entertain the thought of selling our own silver.'

'I'm only suggesting,' said Basil Bradley

25

steadily, 'that it may be some comfort to know that if the appeal and the Festival do not raise the money then at least we have the chalice behind us, as it were.'

'Quite wrong!' said Mrs Mawne forcefully, jamming on her gloves. 'The chalice must remain here for future generations.'

'Absolutely!' growled Major Gunning.

'Let's hope it won't come to that,' said Mr Roberts. 'We'll do our best to get the cash in every other way possible.'

And on that note, the meeting ended.

*   *   *

Later that night, the vicar lay sleepless, watching the moonlight wavering upon the ceiling above his head. Somewhere, far away, a stoat yelped shrilly. The leaves of the Virginia creeper rustled by the open window, and near at hand his big silver watch ticked companionably from the bedside table.

All was as usual in the peaceful room, but still sleep evaded him.

His thoughts turned again and again to Henry's appalling suggestion. How could he have conceived such an idea? It amounted almost to betrayal. The whole idea was monstrous. He simply could not think what Henry meant by putting forward such an outrageous scheme. It was bad enough to have had such thoughts. To put them into words

26

made the matter even worse! The poor vicar tossed restlessly, and remembered the beauty of the ancient chalice with piercing clarity.

How heavy and smooth it was to handle! How comforting was the sturdy stem, the beautiful moulded base! How warm and glowing the red wine looked in its polished depths! To the vicar, and to his flock, Queen Anne's chalice, as it was known, was a precious part of the Christmas and Easter communion service. And had been, the vicar reminded himself, for generation upon generation of Fairacre folk. Lips, dusty-dead two hundred years and more, had sipped the wine from this cup. Squire and servant, man and maid, the virtuous and the villainous had knelt beside each other awaiting pardon and peace from the chalice.

And they would do so still, the vicar told himself resolutely. They would do so still!

He turned over his pillow, thumped it soundly as though he trounced the Devil himself, and was asleep in three minutes.

CHAPTER THREE

The autumn was wet, windy and unseasonably warm. The children squelched into school from muddy lanes and the puddle-filled playground, incurring the wrath of Mrs Pringle daily.

Scaffolding was beginning to shroud the stumpy spire of St Patrick's and the damaged area of the nave, and the Appeal Fund board made a new feature in the village. So far the hand of the clock on the board stood only at one hundred and twenty-three pounds, but as we all pointed out to each other, it was a wonderful beginning.

The weathervane had been removed and the cock awaited regilding. On the day it was brought down to ground level Mr Willet put his head round the school door.

'If you've got a minute to spare,' he said deferentially, 'you might like a close look at the ol' weathercock. He's come to roost in the churchyard, afore he gets a new lick of paint.'

The children began clamouring at once, only too glad to leave their English exercises.

'We'll come straightaway,' I told Mr Willet, rising in readiness to quell the stampede to the door. When we had attained some semblance of order we made our way decorously to the churchyard. Near the south door, propped against a convenient flat tombstone, stood St Patrick's weathercock. It was surprisingly large with an expression of great ferocity.

'It's bigger'n our baby,' breathed Joseph Coggs with awe, stroking its cold head with a grimy hand.

'Weighs a fair bit, too,' said one of the workmen. 'Plenty of good metal in him.'

The children surveyed it admiringly and a few of them seated themselves on the damp tombstone beside it.

'Get up! Don't sit there!' I said a trifle sharply, more concerned with internal chills than irreverence, I must confess.

'Old Tom wouldn't mind, miss,' said Mr Willet peaceably. 'A loving sort of man by all accounts, specially to children—or so his stone do say.'

I stood rebuked in the face of such tolerance. A few yellow leaves fluttered down upon the sodden grass, and a wren skittered up and down the hawthorn hedge by the lych gate. Sunshine, so seldom seen in the last few drenching weeks, flooded the scene with amber light.

'We'll go for a walk before going back to school,' I announced, amidst general rejoicing. Thanks were given to Mr Willet and the workmen, affectionate pats to the weathercock, and then we set off to profit from sweet country air and exercise, in the forlorn hope that they would sharpen our wits for the work awaiting us in the schoolroom.

As Christmas approached, the money-raising activities increased in the village. The Fur and Feather Whist Drive was well attended, and the usual display of turkeys, ducks, hens, pheasants, and hares adorned the platform in the village hall. Almost thirty pounds was raised by this mammoth effort, and only the collapse of the trestle table bearing the coffee cups marred the success of the evening.

'And it's my belief,' Mrs Pringle told me the next morning, 'that Mrs Emery's ugly great dog pushed the legs along. No business to let an animal into the hall at all. Nothing but a bag of fleas and smelling worse nor Mr Roberts's pigs! As I told her straight.'

Mrs Pringle is a great one for 'telling people straight' and makes much trouble in doing so. Sometimes I feel like quoting to her a prayer learned in childhood which says: 'Let me not mistake bluntness for frankness,' but I doubt if such a frail dart would penetrate my school cleaner's rhinoceros' hide. And as she herself is so fond of saying: 'You can't teach an old dog new tricks.' I have learnt to leave well alone whenever possible, for Mrs Pringle makes a formidable foe, and I have to meet her daily.

We spent the latter weeks of the term preparing a school play, in which every child from the smallest five-year-old to Ernest, a hefty eleven-year-old, had a part. Miss Clare, who once taught the infants' class at Fairacre, emerged from her retirement at Beech Green to help to dress the children and to play the accompaniment to their songs. The parents packed the school to overflowing, and apart from such expected crises as a measles suspect, two sore throats, a burst knicker elastic and a hitch in the curtain-pulling equipment, it all went splendidly. Two performances of our masterpiece netted ten pounds for the fund, and we were well content.

'A Gigantic Christmas Bazaar' widely advertised by posters on barns, trees and gateposts, as well as a notice in the *Caxley Chronicle*, was perhaps a trifle larger than the usual Christmas Bazaar which Fairacre organizes, and we all bought knitted tea-cosies and gingham aprons for each other's Christmas presents, and little boxes of homemade fudge which we fully intended to give away too, but ate ourselves as it was quite irresistible and, as we told ourselves, might not keep. The Appeal Fund was larger by twenty-six pounds at the end of the afternoon.

Nevertheless, the hand moved very slowly towards the target of two thousand pounds. After morning service on Christmas Day a little knot of us stood outside the church, in the bleak east wind, exchanging Christmas greetings and discussing the progress of the Appeal. The hand pointed to a little under four hundred pounds, and with the best will in the world it was hard to be very optimistic.

'I suppose it's not too bad for a beginning,' said Miss Margaret Waters to her sister Mary. 'After all, it's only a few weeks since it happened.'

'I'd like to see it nearer the thousand,' said Mr Willet, standing next to her. 'We've had in the best part of the donations, from all accounts. Once we gets into the New Year, somehow it won't seem so urgent. People soon forgets, you know.'

Mrs Pringle, emerging after her stentorian boomings in the choir, heard the last part of Mr Willet's remarks.

'"Forgets" is the word, Mr Willet. Why, in the old days, this money would've been found in next to no time. The gentry—who *was* gentry then, let me say—would have put their hands in their pockets and settled it at once.'

'There ain't the money about,' agreed Mr Willet. 'At least, not to the same extent. It's spread over a few more, that's all, and them as earns it sticks to it. You can't blame the gentry. The tax man gets it off of them, and there's nothing left for things like the church spire.'

We gazed dolefully aloft at the roof, now bristling with scaffolding. No bells had rung a Christmas peal this year, because of the damage in the belfry. St Patrick's wore a forlorn and battered air. Without its golden weathercock the little spire looked unusually truncated.

'Ah well!' said Mr Willet, turning up his coat collar against the wind, 'mustn't lose heart, you know, specially on Christmas Day! Maybe, the New Year will bring us all a bit of luck. And there's always the Festival to look forward to!'

'Yes, indeed,' said Mary Waters, snatching at this comfort. 'There's always the Festival!'

We set off on our several ways determined to be of good cheer, despite the nagging little doubts which pierced our defences as keenly as the bleak east wind about us.

The Christmas holidays slipped away with their usual speed and the spring term began in a flurry of snow. The children, of course greeted it with rapture. Mrs Pringle looked upon it as yet another cross to bear. She went about her duties tight-lipped and with the limp which becomes more marked when she feels more than usually 'put upon'.

Luckily, the snow was light, nothing more than a shower here and there, powdering the black branches of the elms and the roofs in the village. But the weather was bitterly cold and even I, a poor weather prophet, knew that we should get more snow before long.

On one freezing evening the Festival Committee met in my sitting-room. Thanks to Mrs Pringle's administrations it presented an unusually tidy appearance. Piles of exercise books, test papers, infant apparatus and the general flotsam and jetsam found in a school-mistress's room had been carted up to the spare bedroom, and although I despaired of ever finding any of it in order again, it was wonderful to entertain my guests in such immaculate splendour.

The Committee was formed by most of the Parochial Church Council and one or two other energetic people who had some organizing ability and bright ideas. I must confess that I had envisaged an evening making a list of the usual entertainments known only too well to Fairacre, and possibly deciding on the days on which to present them. It was exciting therefore to have Basil Bradley's bombshell exploded at the outset.

'This is really Major Gunning's idea,' he began, glancing across at that upright figure. 'You remember that he suggested that we might have *Son et Lumière* with St Patrick's as the background. Well, I've been talking to a friend of mine who has helped to produce this sort of thing, and he's willing to stage it and produce it for us.'

Congratulatory murmurs broke out on all sides.

'And if you would allow me,' went on Basil Bradley, looking modestly at his fingers, 'I should really love to write the story and—er— record it for you.'

'That is indeed most generous,' said the vicar. 'Most generous.'

We all agreed warmly. It was Mrs Mawne who rushed in where angels feared to tread, and said:

'But all that wiring and amplifiers, and setting up seats and things in the churchyard— surely that's going to be horribly expensive?'

'I thought, if the vicar agreed, it would be much more practical to have it inside the church, with the lights changing on the chancel

34

and altar. Then, of course, we should be independent of the weather.'

'And have seats,' cried Mrs Mawne, seeing the light.

'And have seats,' agreed Basil Bradley gravely.

'I can see no objection to having the performances inside,' said the vicar. 'After all, the churches were always used for the early miracle plays, and it seems fitting that the story of our parish should be told in the building which has seen almost all its history. I think it is a splendid idea.'

'The only thing is,' said Basil Bradley, warming to his theme in the midst of such general approval, 'it is hardly worth setting up all the paraphernalia for less than a week. Do you think we can expect enough support?'

'Why not?' asked Mr Mawne. 'We'll advertise it well. People can bring parties from miles away. They're much more likely to come if they know it will be inside the building.'

'Oh, I do agree,' said his wife firmly. 'What with gnats, and the wind, not to mention the odd thunderstorm, outdoor evenings are more of a penance than a pleasure.'

It was at last agreed that the *Son et Lumière* arrangements would be for every evening of the Festival Week, and would, in fact, be the major part of the whole project which would take place in July.

'And do you really think we shall cover our

35

expenses?' persisted Mrs Mawne.

'There will be no expenses,' said Basil Bradley. 'My friend John is giving his services, and the electrician's bills and so on will be my own contribution to the Fund.'

'It is uncommonly generous,' repeated the vicar. 'A really wonderful gesture. I am sure we are most deeply grateful.' And with this we all concurred.

Major Gunning cleared his throat so martially that we all jumped to attention, or as nearly as we could in a sitting posture.

'I've taken the liberty of speaking to a young cousin of mine . . . by way of being a singer. You may have heard of her. Jean Cole.'

'Jean Cole!' exclaimed Mrs Mawne, looking at Major Gunning with new respect.

'Jean Cole!' echoed Basil Bradley, turning pink with excitement. 'I'd no idea she was related to you. The most beautiful contralto voice in existence today! She was superb in *Aïda* at Covent Garden last year.'

'I have all her records,' said the vicar. 'The Bach arias are my particular favourites.'

Major Gunning bowed his head politely in acknowledgement of the adulation, but his tobacco-stained fingers, drumming on the edge of the table, showed his impatience.

'Yes, well . . . top and bottom of it is that she would be willing to give us a tune . . .'

Basil Bradley winced.

'To come here? To Fairacre?' breathed Mrs

36

Mawne incredulously.

'As I was saying,' continued Major Gunning with a touch of asperity, 'Jean said that she could come and sing in the church during, or after, the *Son et Lumière* performance, if it would help. Not the Monday, though. She's flying back from Berlin that day, after a tour.'

There were delighted cries from the company. The vicar broached the delicate subject which was in all our minds.

'It is indeed the most generous offer. It would mean a great deal to our efforts. But your cousin is—er—much in demand. We must offer her some—er—recompense for the honour she is doing us. Can we . . . ?'

'She'll come,' said the major briefly, 'for nothing. I'll see to that.'

If this sounded a trifle ominous, it was soon forgotten in the general delight.

'It's too good to be true,' cried Mrs Mawne. 'The most encouraging news of the evening!'

And with that we all agreed.

The rest of the programme was settled provisionally. The *Son et Lumière* would take place after dark each evening, beginning about nine. The Festival would begin with a splendid service in the church on the Sunday, at which the Bishop had promised to come and bless our endeavours.

'And all denominations in the area will be invited,' said the vicar.

'Bet they don't all come!' whispered Mr

37

Roberts to me in a horribly penetrating whisper.

'They will be invited,' repeated the vicar reprovingly.

Various functions would take place during the week, a mammoth jumble sale, a gargantuan whist drive and so on, organized by various bodies in the village, and the week would culminate with a magnificent fête in the vicarage garden on Saturday afternoon, to be opened by someone who would be 'a real draw', as Mr Willet said, followed by a dance in the evening.

'Shall we have enough going on to warrant a *whole week*?' asked Mr Willet doubtfully.

'The *Son et Lumière* will be the main thread,' explained the vicar, 'and our other festivities will be hung like jewels, as it were, upon this chain.'

'Very nicely put,' commented Mr Mawne, a trifle drily.

'Yes, it turned out rather more poetically than I intended,' replied the vicar, rather surprised and pleased with his flight of fancy. 'I really should make a note of it for a future sermon.'

By this time the hands of the clock stood at ten o'clock. I went into the kitchen to prepare coffee, and the meeting ended with much animation and hope, on the part of the Fairacre Festival Committee, before they set off to face the wintry night.

CHAPTER FOUR

'No, I never!'

'Yes, you did then!'

'I never, I tell you! I never done it!'

'We knows you done it all right, don't us?'

A chorus of self-righteous voices greeted this ungrammatical exchange which floated through the schoolroom window one bright morning. Sometimes I wonder why I trouble to correct the children in the classroom, knowing full well that they will relapse into their mother tongue as soon as they escape from my clutches.

The accused appeared to be Joseph Coggs. I could recognize his hoarse, husky croak easily above the manifold sounds from the playground. He is fairly popular with the other children who do not seem to be bothered by his poor clothes and his gipsy background. What he had done to deserve their united attack I was soon to know.

' 'Twas there all right yesterday,' said one, belligerently.

'Funny thing you havin' a wooden dagger the same evenin',' shouted another mockingly.

'My cousin from Caxley give it to me,' growled Joseph. 'He got it off of some kid up the street.'

'Likely, ennit?'

39

'What, same colour an' all?'

The voices grew shriller, and I was in half a mind to leave my marking to investigate when I heard Mr Willet's hearty voice.

'What's going on then?'

A dozen voices clamoured together, and the gist of the story was that the hand of the clock had vanished from the Appeal Fund and Joseph Coggs 'had bin and pinched it'.

'You want to watch your tongues,' announced Mr Willet sternly. 'And stop picking on Joe. I took the hand away, if you must know, to put another coat o' paint on it. Put that in your pipes and smoke it, you young know-alls.'

His heavy footsteps passed on, leaving an uneasy silence.

'See?' cried Joseph triumphantly.

'Well, how was we to know?' muttered one of the crowd. 'Your dagger was the spittin' image of that hand.'

'Always on at us to look out for folks breakin' the law,' grumbled another, 'and what thanks do us get for trying?'

'Come on up the coke-heap,' shouted someone cheerfully. 'The bell'll be going before we've had a game.'

And the drama ended in a wild confusion of yells and scrunching coke, enjoyed by accusers and accused alike.

*   *   *

The hand of the clock which had been the cause of this fracas was moving far too slowly towards the target for Fairacre's peace of mind.

The most dramatic leap forward, in these last months, had been caused by an anonymous gift of one hundred pounds. Naturally, rumours as to the identity of this generous benefactor were legion.

'I wouldn't put it past the vicar himself,' said one.

'Or Mr Mawne?' queried another.

'That'll be the day,' said Mrs Pringle sourly, when she heard this suggestion. 'Them Mawnes don't part with money that easy. Best end of neck served up as chops in their house, so my niece Minnie tells me.'

One of the infants thought it might be 'a fairy'. This pretty fancy was soon dispelled by the realists who were slightly older.

'Don't talk soft!' implored her brother Ernest, shamed before his fellows in the playground.

'No such thing as fairies,' added Patrick scornfully. 'And if there was, how d'you think they'd lug a hundred pounds up to the vicar's? They ain't no bigger'n my thumb.'

This irrefutable argument settled the matter, in this instance, but the anonymous donor still remained a fascinating mystery. It was one which was never solved.

Even more exciting than the anonymous gift was that Peter Martin, the pop star and idol of the young, had agreed to open the fête on the Saturday and to sing at the dance in the evening, accompanying himself on the famous guitar. He was going to prove a tremendous draw.

'The weather really won't matter,' said the vicar, beaming. 'People will come from miles around just to see him. A very *personable* young fellow, I believe.'

Mrs Pringle's niece Minnie expressed the general reaction to the news.

'Ain't it just wonderful? We'll be breathing *the very same air*! To think of him coming to this place! All Caxley'll be there. You ever seen him, miss?'

I said that I had not had that pleasure yet.

'Beautiful hair, he's got. Long and that, all thick down to his shoulders. And his clothes costs a fortune, and he don't drink nothin' but champagne!'

She sighed ecstatically. A visitation from the entire heavenly host, I thought somewhat tartly to myself, could not occasion more reverent adoration than this one glamorous star. Nevertheless, I too rejoiced. Think how it would swell the funds!

Work on the roof progressed steadily, and the sound of hammers and saws formed the background to our own school activities. These included now, in the last weeks of the spring

42

term, preparations for the entertainment which was to be our contribution to the Fairacre Festival.

Only teachers, who have dealt with these affairs, can truly assess the heart-burnings and headaches which accompany something which the outsider considers a simple, and even a pleasurable, undertaking.

The only other member of the staff is the infants' teacher. For years Miss Clare, now retired and living at Beech Green, ruled the infants, and most of the adults in the village learned to read, write and calculate under her benevolent eye. Miss Gray followed Miss Clare, but left to marry our neighbouring schoolmaster, Mr Annett, who also acts as choirmaster and organist at Fairacre. Then came Miss Jackson, a stormy young woman straight from college whose departure I viewed with relief.

Since then we have had a succession of 'supply' teachers, some good, some ghastly; but for the last year the infants have been in the charge of Mrs Bonny, a buxom widow, who manages them very well. All goes swimmingly if she is able to work in her own way, and I interfere as little as possible. Unfortunately, any sort of mild suggestion throws the lady into a defensive and resentful mood, as if one were casting a slur on her abilities. Coming to an amicable arrangement about the concert was an operation fraught with hazards, I found.

My first idea of a play in which the whole school could take part fell upon stony ground.

'Why can't the babies sing their nursery rhymes?' demanded Mrs Bonny plaintively. 'I've spent hours teaching them, and their mothers would love to hear them.'

Both facts were true. The daily chorus—one might be forgiven for saying 'caterwauling'— had penetrated the partition between our classrooms with painful clarity. And the mothers of these young choristers would dote on Mrs Bonny's efforts with them. I agreed resignedly.

'But nursery rhymes won't take very long,' I said, trying not to sound too relieved. 'We'd better have some other items.'

Mrs Bonny promised to consider the matter, and within two days the floorboards of the infants' room were reverberating with one of those galumphing folk dances from mid-Europe which involve much clapping and stamping. The clapping and stamping are no doubt performed in unison in the country of the dance's origin, but it certainly was not in Fairacre's infant room. Next door we were sorely tried. It was almost a relief to return to the nursery rhymes, and to listen, wincing, to:

'Ickory, dickory dock
The mou-house run up the clock
The clock struck ONE

The mouse run down—

Here there followed a succession of claps as each child took its time to register the need for action, and then, triumphantly they would bellow:

'Ickory, dickory, dock.

Mrs Bonny would then praise them loudly, point out the aspirate at the beginning of 'Hickory' and the necessity of singing 'ran' instead of 'run', and the same thing would be repeated *ad nauseam*.

Our own efforts were little better. I had dramatized *The Princess and the Swineherd*, which gave everyone a chance of appearing on the stage, and doubted if the words would ever be learnt. Ernest, the only possible swineherd-cum-prince, became so sheepish about performing a courtly bow that I threatened to demote him to a courtier, although we both knew that there was no one else really capable of taking the part. Sometimes I despaired of ever getting Fairacre School to take part in the Festival, and wondered gloomily if the sale of Queen Anne's chalice might not, after all, be a better way of raising the money.

I did not, of course, voice these treacherous sentiments, but Mr Lamb, our village postmaster, spoke about it when I went to buy the school's savings' stamps one afternoon,

45

some weeks later.

'Of course, it's not plain sailing, this selling the church silver. Has to be a Faculty or something, the vicar tells me. A lot of chit-chat goes on evidently before permission's given. I can't see us being allowed to part with it. And, to tell the truth, I don't think anyone in Fairacre wants to see it go.'

He handed me the stamps and with them three or four photographs in colour.

'Your brother's family?' I asked, looking at them. Mr Lamb's brother George left Fairacre for New York after the war and runs a catering business there. He left before I took over the school but regularly corresponds with our Mr Lamb who shows us the photographs, and tells us all about his brother's successes, when we visit the Post Office. He is very proud indeed of this younger brother, now the father of three husky boys who beamed from the photographs.

'Just a chance he may be over,' said Mr Lamb, taking back the photographs and inserting them carefully into his wallet. 'Some business trip, he says. They're chartering a plane, it seems, and if he can manage it, he'll be over here for a fortnight.'

This was good news. As I sauntered down the village street, enjoying the sunshine, I hoped, for Mr Lamb's sake, that his brother would be able to return to Fairacre. It was my guess that he would not find it much changed even though he had been absent now for over twenty years.

The question of the sale of the chalice was in everyone's mind. None worried quite as deeply as the vicar. He woke, on these bright summer mornings, to the chorus of the birds in his garden and then, after the first few moments of pleasure, the familiar little cloud cooled the sunshine of his waking moments and was with him for the rest of the day. He refused to do anything about negotiations for the sale of the precious chalice. He steadfastly hoped and prayed that enough would be raised by the Festival, and that this step, so repugnant to him, might never be necessary.

Mr Mawne did his best to make his friend change his mind, but he remained obdurate.

'I refuse to discuss it,' said the vicar one evening, pink with rare impatience.

'But, my dear Gerald, you simply can't bury your head in the sand like an ostrich. At least find out the facts. Let's see if we can try for permission. Time's running out, you know. The bills are going to be pretty formidable, and can you honestly believe that the Festival will raise enough to pay them?'

'I have no doubt that the Lord will provide,' repeated the vicar stubbornly. His friend raised his eyebrows, looked helplessly at Mrs Partridge, but forbore to reply.

The chalice had last been used at Whitsun, and not one touching the ancient mellow silver and gazing into its gleaming depths failed to feel a pang. Would this be the last time that Fairacre's treasure, with its blessed contents, would be offered to them? The service was a paean of praise. Red and white roses nodded on the altar. Sunshine poured through the windows, gilding the arum lilies at the chancel steps. Country voices had made the glittering brass vibrate with Whitsun hymns and Mr Annett, at the organ, had pulled out all the stops and flooded the church with mighty splendour. The thought of the possible loss of the chalice was the one touch of frost among the bursting glory of Whit Sunday.

As the Festival drew closer our fears for the chalice became sharper. Somehow we simply must make the Fairacre Festival a success, we told each other! We did not say, in so many words, that Queen Anne's chalice was at stake, but the unspoken thought was constantly with us.

It was Mrs Pringle, usually the harbinger of doom, who brought a rare touch of comfort to Mr Partridge, the vicar, at about this time. He had called at the school with the list of hymns which he hoped I would teach the children, when Mrs Pringle clattered in bearing a battered pail in one hand and a scrubbing brush in the other.

'Bit late leavin', ain't you?' she remarked sourly. 'Clock wrong then? I was going to give the lobby a scrub out but no use doing it till the children have cleared off. Love's labour lost, that'd be!'

The vicar, who is used to this sort of thing, smiled benignly.

'You're going to have a churchful on the Tuesday then. You was lucky to get that Miss Cole to sing,' she continued conversationally, setting down the bucket with a clang. 'My sister's girl, what works at the coach station in Caxley, says there's three coach loads booked already to come over,'

The vicar's smile grew wider.

'What splendid news, Mrs Pringle!'

'And no end of Women's Institutes have rung up about it, and the Mothers' Union and some Young Farmers.'

'A really *wide* audience!' commented the vicar rapturously.

'It takes all sorts to make a world,' conceded Mrs Pringle graciously. 'But it do look hopeful, I must say.'

'It does indeed,' replied the vicar, gazing affectionately upon my school cleaner. 'It does indeed.'

She bent to pick up the bucket and then took up her customary militant stance.

'Well,' she demanded, with a return to her usual truculence, 'do them children go now or not? This 'ere water's getting cold.'

'I'll send them through the other way,' I said meekly. 'We won't hold up your scrubbing any longer.'

This was no time for petty warfare, I felt. Mrs Pringle, messenger of hope, should have her way.

CHAPTER FIVE

The posters were up everywhere in the countryside. They blazed from barn doors, from gateposts, from tree trunks and in the windows of many a village shop. One made a bright blue corner on the Appeals' board. Across the village street, between 'The Beetle and Wedge' and the Emerys' house, a banner fluttered, bearing the words:

FAIRACRE FESTIVAL
JULY 9–15

Bunting was draped across our house fronts, and those of us who owned a flag had it in readiness to hoist on the Sunday which was to be the first day of the Festival. The cross of St George, freshly laundered by Mrs Willet, would soon be flaunting itself above the church spire upon which the regilded weathercock perched again.

Inside the church the electricians were putting the final touches to the wiring and lighting. Jock Graham, the retired architect who had so nobly offered his services, became

50

extremely agitated by the ladders lodged among the timbers of the hammerbeam roof. He was unduly sharp with Mr Mawne who had dropped in one morning to see how things were progressing.

'I'll not be responsible,' he rumbled, rolling his r's in Doric splendour, 'for any damage to that historic roof. A lot of tomfoolery to rig up lights so near the timbers. Those men have no idea of the pricelessness of the work around them.'

'Oh, come now,' protested Mr Mawne. 'They are used to this sort of thing. I believe they were employed at Winchester Cathedral. Or was it Salisbury?'

'It wouldn't be allowed in Scotland,' Mr Graham assured him.

'That I can well imagine,' remarked his companion drily. The hint of sarcasm inflamed Jock Graham still further.

'A decent God-fearing kirk would be ashamed to turn itself into something no better than a theatre. I'd no idea, when I offered my sairvices, that this sort of thing would be countenanced.'

'I see nothing offensive about it,' retorted Mr Mawne. 'It is an act of praise.'

'It's commaircial!' boomed Mr Graham, his sandy eyebrows bristling. 'It wouldn't happen in Scotland, I tell ye!'

'I really can't think,' replied Mr Mawne, with maddening detachment, 'why so many of

51

you Scotsmen bother to come south if you dislike it so much. Personally, I'm all for Scottish nationalism, and I'd rebuild Hadrian's Wall for good measure, once I'd got all you immigrants back on the right side of it.'

'Ye'd no get far without a stiffening of good Scots' blood among ye,' thundered Jock Graham. 'A weakly unprincipled set of shilly-shallyers, lacking pairpose and integrity!'

The workmen, high above, had ceased their labours and were watching this passage of arms with intense interest.

The two men faced each other. Mr Mawne's pale face wore a supercilious smile. Mr Graham's, suffused to an unbecoming shade of purple, was thrust close to his antagonist's. At this dramatic moment, Basil Bradley arrived on the scene.

'I can't tell you how relieved I am that I've already recorded the script,' he croaked huskily. 'My tonsils are absolutely aflame. I can't think why I've succumbed so easily at this time of year. I swear by orange juice for breakfast—nothing more—just fresh orange juice!'

'Ye'd do better on a braw fresh herring and a plate of salted porridge,' thundered Jock Graham. He brushed past the two men and marched, head erect, down the aisle to the west door.

'Whatever's got into him?' asked Basil Bradley, bewildered.

'Scotch blood,' said Mr Mawne cryptically. '"Scotland for ever!" I mean "Scotland for aye!"'

'Oh dear,' croaked Basil Bradley, extracting a small tin from his pocket. 'Ah well, it makes one quite glad to have been born in humble Bayswater, doesn't it? Have a blackcurrant lozenge, Henry.'

*   *   *

Jock Graham was not the only Fairacre resident to be in a state of tension at this time. The vicar, facing the Bishop's visit, was anxious about the service, and also about the safety of the church fabric. What a terrible thing it would be if something should fall upon that stately figure! Despite reassurances, the vicar was not wholly at ease. Mrs Partridge, whose privilege it was to entertain the Bishop to lunch, and possibly to tea, was busy planning a meal which would do honour to their distinguished visitor and yet be simple enough to prepare and serve single-handed. Cold salmon and salad had seemed a good choice until she remembered that the Bishop was extremely short-sighted and far too handsome a man to relish wearing glasses at lunch time. And just suppose that a fish-bone appeared? It would, without fail, be on the guest's plate. Perhaps cold beef? Or leg of lamb left in a slow oven during the service and mint sauce made beforehand?

Mrs Partridge continued to cudgel her brains, and to long for the days when the vicarage had a resident cook and two kitchen maids.

Mr Annett, the choir master, was worrying about the new anthem. The choir of St Patrick's had left him in no doubt that he had bitten off more than they could chew.

'This 'ere modern stuff ain't got no tune to it,' protested Mr Willet. 'What's wrong with a bit of Bach or Handel?'

'It's a very good thing to make a change,' Mr Annett snapped back, secretly conscious that the new anthem was beyond their powers, but too proud to admit it. 'As Browning said:

A man's reach should exceed his grasp.'

'Browning never 'ad to tackle this lot,' pointed out Mr Willet, peering closely at the sheet of music. 'If there's anything I 'ates it's five flats.'

They had struggled on with their unfamiliar burden, but no matter how often they practised, Mr Annett realized that the anthem would turn out to be a hesitant dirge rather than the outpouring of praise which the composer had intended. Too late to do anything now, he told himself, as the great Sunday approached. But the thought gave him little comfort.

Basil Bradley, afflicted with his feverish

cold, was suffering agonies of self-consciousness about the script which he had written, and his recording of it. He had checked all his facts most carefully, but there was always the possibility of a mistake. How dreadful if he had made some blunder! There was that episode about the nun being given shelter in the vestry during the eighteenth century. Should he have omitted it, perhaps? There were some very dubious rumours about the incumbent at that date, and the Bishop might take exception to the publicity, guarded though Basil's account had been of the affair. Really, creative work was terribly exhausting, thought poor Basil, as he gargled hopelessly before the final rehearsal.

A spell of unbroken sunshine preceded Festival week and we in Fairacre prayed that it might continue. It grew so hot that the children took many of their lessons outside, in the shade of the elm trees. Rehearsals of the infants' contributions also took place in the playground, which afforded some relief to our class, when it was working inside, and considerable interest to proud mothers who clustered at the gate to watch their offspring bounding around in the folk dance.

The Princess and the Swineherd still had many faults. Ernest had overcome his shyness with such success—terrified of handing over the part to someone else—that he now played the Prince with a swashbuckling impudence which was, to my mind, quite as offensive as his former interpretation of the part. However, I was now resigned to the shortcomings of my production and simply concentrated on getting the cast word-perfect, which was no light matter.

Mr Willet, as sexton, was concerned about the tidiness of the church and the churchyard.

'Slummocky lot, them builders,' he told me. 'Drops their paper bags everywhere. Bread crusts and cheese rinds and old potato crisps scattered all over the churchyard. Them mice are getting as big as foxes.'

'It will look splendid on Sunday,' I assured him. 'Especially if this weather lasts.'

We looked across my garden to the meadows at the base of the downs. A heat haze veiled the distance, but nearer at hand a herd of black and white Friesian cows, the pride of Mr Roberts, stood knee-deep in tall grass. Not one moved. They might have been painted there, against the hot motionless beauty of hills and empty sky, so still they stood.

'Well, let's hope it does,' agreed Mr Willet. 'Don't want it to break yet awhile. It'll end in thunder, or my name's not Willet.'

He turned to look at St Patrick's. The scaffolding had been removed from the spire but still clad the square tower containing the belfry and part of the nave.

56

'Wish we could have rung in the Bishop with a fine peal,' he said regretfully. 'But there it is. All six o' they bells is up against the church wall waiting to go aloft again as soon as it's safe for 'em. I likes to go and look 'em over now and again. I've got a soft spot for them bells, particularly Old Bess. They say she was cast in the field behind "The Beetle and Wedge", sometime in the 1560s.'

'The children don't want the bells to go back again. They've been over to see them— under my eagle eye, let me say—lots of times, and they've copied the inscriptions.'

' "Sanctus, sanctus, sanctus",' gabbled Mr Willet, swatting a gnat on his freckled forearm. " 'In piam memoriam Caroli Fowler. Requiescat in pace". Fowler, notice? Still a good few Fowlers in Fairacre. Wonder if any of them cast Old Bess?'

He bent to pull up a dandelion from my border, and straightened up with a sigh.

'I do truly hope this Festival puts the old church on its feet. There's a lot at stake, Miss Read. A lot at stake!'

*   *   *

Sunday dawned bright and beautiful. I took my breakfast tray into the garden among the dewy pinks and roses. A robin perched hopefully on the lilac bush nearby, a beady eye cocked for crumbs.

The Union Jack hung motionless from the school flag pole. High above it, on St Patrick's church the cross of St George waited for a breeze to spread it out in its full red and white magnificence.

It was already blissfully hot although the clock said only nine. By ten to eleven, when I made my way to church, the heat was almost oppressive. We were all in our best summer finery and I felt quite sorry for the Bishop, magnificently accoutred in a splendid gold and white cope which must have been uncomfortably warm.

We sang the most exultant hymns, beginning with 'Praise my soul the King of Heaven' as the choir processed from the west door up to the chancel. Several of my pupils had undergone their weekly metamorphosis from scruffy urchins to well-scrubbed cherubs, and with hair plastered down with a wet brush and their eyes modestly downcast upon the polished boots peeping demurely from beneath their cassocks, they gave an impression of youthful sanctity which did not deceive those of us who knew them during the rest of the week.

The new anthem was tackled with dogged effort and Mr Annett gave noble support not only with his hands and feet at the organ, but with a resonant voice which led his struggling choir valiantly. When it was over, I noticed Mr Willet mopping his brow and moustache with obvious relief.

The Bishop gave the sermon and spoke of the part the church played in parish life, the disaster which had befallen it, and praised the efforts of our small community to repair the damage.

'God will bless your work,' he promised us. 'This is a Festival in every sense. It is an expression of praise for past mercies and a rededication of ourselves to service.'

He made a brave and unforgettable figure in our ancient pulpit, and his words were as inspiring as his presence. When the benediction had been said, and Mr Annett broke into a triumphant voluntary, we all felt that Fairacre was embarked upon a venture which was bound to succeed.

We emerged into the hot sunshine, blinking like owls in the dazzling light. Around us the rose bushes gave out a voluptuous fragrance. Above us an aeroplane left a white trail in the cloudless sky. Bumble bees lumbered from clover-head to clover-head on the grassy mounds of our Fairacre forefathers. It was indeed high summer.

'And real Festival weather!' said Miss Margaret Waters, gazing happily about her, beneath the brim of her old-fashioned straw hat.

'After all this looking forward,' said her sister, 'it's hard to believe that it's actually started.'

It was a thought we all shared as we made our various ways homeward to Sunday dinner.

At last, the Festival had begun!

CHAPTER SIX

Amy my old college friend, drove over from Bent to the first performance of the *Son et Lumière*.

It was to be a very grand affair. Several local landowners were bringing parties of guests and we humbler folk were busy looking out our best evening attire. It was not easy to find something splendid enough for the occasion, decorous enough for churchgoing and warm enough to counteract the chill of an evening in St Patrick's draughty pews. I had plumped for safety in my plain black frock, and had looked out my one fur piece, a useful stole, for despite the heat of the last few days, which had degenerated into an ominously still stuffiness, the age-long coolness of the church's interior would take some combating.

Amy, *soignée* in a most beautiful frock of blue silk, looked me over critically.

'You really *shouldn't* wear black, my dear, with your skin. It kills any sort of glow you have. Why not wear a deep red dress, or a brown?'

'Because I haven't got one,' I said flatly.

Her eye travelled, without relish, down my full length and lingered sadly at my feet.

'Those heels are definitely out,' she pronounced.

'Not in Fairacre,' I replied with spirit. 'In fact, they've only just *come in*! I paid a great deal of money for these shoes, my girl, and I intend to get plenty of wear out of them.'

Amy shuddered delicately, and fingered her one splendid adornment, a glittering diamond brooch on her shoulder. It was, I knew, a present from James, her husband, and marked his return from a particularly protracted business trip to the Bahamas. There are many such absences from home, about which I have my private suspicions, as no doubt Amy has too, but they certainly result in the most beautiful presents for his wife, and she has enough sense not to cross-question James too closely.

We sat down to my carefully prepared meal of cold chicken and salad. I was secretly rather proud of the salad for I had remembered to cut the radishes into water-lily shapes in the dinner hour and had left them soaking all the afternoon. The tomatoes and cucumber had come from Mr Willet's greenhouse, and the lettuce from my own garden. The hard-boiled eggs, winking goldenly from among the greenery, had come from Mrs Pringle's hens and the fine chicken was lately one of the members of her flock.

Amy ate heartily, I was glad to see.

'All so deliciously fresh,' she commented, and I preened myself at this unaccustomed compliment—prematurely, as I might have known.

'But I really think the latest way of dishing up a salad is better. Just a bowl of green stuff tossed in the very best olive oil and vinegar, and tomatoes freshly sliced in a separate dish salted and peppered and with a *soupçon* of chopped chives or parsley, of course—for those who like *coloured* salad mixed with green. I find that most people these days consider radishes rather too coarse a flavour, and there's so much medical argument about hard-boiled eggs that I don't serve them, I must admit.'

'You'd better bring your own nose-bag next time you come,' I told her. I've known Amy too long to worry about her criticisms and can well recall the hearty relish with which she attacked college bread and margarine spread with thick-cut Scottish marmalade, not to mention a truly repellent dish of minced meat in a suet crust which, with juvenile flippancy, we christened 'Boiled Baby'.

However, she approved graciously of my coffee, and as soon as we had finished we set off to the church.

'Looks like thunder,' commented Amy, eyeing the darkening sky. There was a sullen coppery look about the piled clouds, and not a leaf stirred in the airless heat.

'Let's hope it waits until we're safely home again,' I answered, as we joined the queue at the south door.

It was good to see St Patrick's so full. Seldom had the ancient hammerbeam roof looked down upon such a glittering assembly. We had all done our best to make this a splendid occasion. I studied the attire and coiffures around me. There were several new hats, worn by those who felt unable to attend church unless so crowned, and among them was one upon Mrs Pringle's locks. It was entirely new to me. Where was the faithful old number adorned with dangling cherries? Where was the navy-blue, decorated with white feathers, which had first seen the light at her niece Minnie's wedding? No doubt safely lodged on top of the wardrobe at home. I hoped so. I missed those two old friends, but studied the new creation with interest. It was of green straw, formidably brimmed, and garlanded with plastic anemones which looked suspiciously like those given away recently with packets of soap powder. It was exceedingly handsome, I thought, and proof of Mrs Pringle's support of the Festival.

In the front pews sat our local gentry, elegant in silks and velvets, their hair blue-rinsed, silver-streaked, or discreetly tinted. Occasionally, wafts of delicious perfume floated back to us, as a stole was rearranged or

63

a handbag was opened.

The nave was shadowy, but a shaft of golden light illuminated the chancel and altar. Mr Annett, at the organ, played some gentle melody, vaguely familiar, which I guessed must be by Haydn or Mozart.

St Patrick's clock struck nine. The music stopped and the vicar appeared at the chancel steps.

'You are about to hear the story of Fairacre,' he told us, 'and in particular the story of this lovely old church. But before it begins let us pray that we may see it restored to its former beauty, so that those who come after us may cherish it as we have done.'

We slipped to our knees and listened to the simple prayer. Then, with a susurration of silks and satins, we resumed our seats, eager for what might come.

*   *   *

The golden light which suffused the chancel changed to a dim blue. The cross glimmered upon the altar amidst the ghostly shadows. We shivered in awe. It was very quiet. Only, far away, a faint rumbling could be heard. It could have been distant thunder, or a farm vehicle out late upon its lawful business.

There was a faint crackling sound and then Basil Bradley's voice echoed strongly through the church.

'Long, long ago, so learned men tell us, the Romans may have passed this way. They did not settle here as far as we know. Among our downs water is scarce, and there are few natural defences against the elements or the enemy. The Romans left no signs of occupation here.

'But centuries later, when the next invaders came to Britain, they left their mark upon this place. Upon this spot, where now we are gathered, the Normans built a small, strong church of which parts still remain.'

At this point the chancel arch was thrown into prominence, a mellow golden light illuminating the angular stone carving. Few of Fairacre's parishioners had realized until this dramatic moment what unsuspected richness had lain in the shadowy chancel arch so high above them.

'The work was begun probably about the middle of the twelfth century—' A crackling noise interrupted the mellifluous voice, and was immediately followed by a burst of thunder which broke around us like machine-gun fire. We ducked involuntarily at the report, then, remembering ourselves, sat up and looked polite and attentive.

The church was plunged in darkness and the voice had ceased. A little agitated whispering rustled round the congregation.

'Lord Almighty!' boomed Mr Roberts whose voice is as large as his generous heart.

65

'We've been and got struck!'

At this, commotion broke out on all sides. There was nothing panic-stricken about us. We are all used to storms, which can occur with horrifying ferocity, but they are soon over in Fairacre. What really worried us was the breakdown of the performance and the bitter disappointment of all those who had spent so long in preparing it.

The vicar, rising from his seat to direct and comfort his flock, suddenly saw, with amazing clarity, in his mind's eye Queen Anne's chalice. It seemed to float in mid-air, brilliantly clear at first, but gradually fading, as if it were passing away from him to distances unknown. The vicar's heart beat uncomfortably loudly, his throat grew constricted, but he put his fears from him and addressed his flock.

'Please remain seated, dear people. Candles will be lit at once, and would Mr Roberts be so kind as to step across to the vicarage and telephone the Electricity Board to see what can be done?'

'I'm on my way, sir,' called Mr Roberts, and the crash of strong footsteps confirmed this.

'Mark my words,' said Amy beside me. '*The Caxley Chronicle* will tell us that this power cut was caused by a swan flying into the cable.'

'Perhaps it was,' I replied.

'Fiddlesticks!' snapped Amy. 'It was the storm!'

A jagged flash split the sky, to be followed

66

by another reverberating thunder clap.

'It's farther off,' said someone hopefully.

'You wants to count, one, two, three, four, see? As soon as the lightning comes you starts counting and sees how many you gets to afore the thunder bangs out. That'll tell you how many miles off the storm be!'

I recognized the voice of this young know-all as Ernest, my Swineherd-Prince.

'You speak when you're spoken to,' said his mother, in a scandalized whisper. 'Piping up like that, and in church, too!'

A few scurrying figures flitted about the shadows bearing candles. There was a medieval beauty about their downbent heads and their curved hands sheltering the precious tiny flames from any draught, which was poignantly in keeping with the ancient building.

'Mr Annett,' announced the vicar, 'will play some music by Bach while we wait.'

We settled back against the hard pew-backs and let the sonorous chords flow over us. How many of our Fairacre forebears, I wondered, had listened to Bach by candlelight, as we were doing now? My mind began to wander. There was something wonderfully comforting in the thought that we shared so much in this building with those long-dead and those yet unborn. We were, after all, simply a link in a long chain stretching back for centuries and forward into eternity.

The candle flames stretched and wavered in the draught. A rumble of thunder rattled over the roof.

'I told you so,' whispered Ernest defensively. 'It's going away.'

At that moment, Mr Roberts reappeared.

'The power will be back at any minute,' he announced. 'A swan has flown into the cable, they say.'

Amy nudged me with such vigour that my side was quite sore.

'Thank you, Mr Roberts,' said the vicar 'Let us sing a hymn together while we wait.'

After some whispering with Mr Annett, the vicar proclaimed:

'Pleasant are thy courts above' and we all dutifully arose in the twilit church and raised our voices. As we reached the last line, the lights came on again, and we sang 'Amen' with undue fervour.

We resumed our seats expectantly and Basil Bradley, looking slightly careworn, appeared at the chancel steps.

'I think we had better begin again from the beginning, ladies and gentlemen. We are so very sorry for this breakdown. Please bear with us, and let us hope that all is now plain sailing.'

There were sympathetic murmurs from the congregation, the lights went out and the blue spotlight lit up the altar once more. There was a preliminary crackle and then Basil Bradley's voice as before.

'Long, long ago, so learned men tell us, the Romans may have passed this way.'

We settled back, like children hungry for a story, and gave ourselves up to enjoyment.

* * *

It took a little over an hour for the tale to unfold, and so well had Basil Bradley told it and so beautiful had the lighting been, that we emerged from the experience filled with unbounded admiration tinged with awe.

Even Amy was impressed.

'*Remarkably* good,' she said as we walked home. 'Really *outstandingly* good! It ought to bring hundreds of visitors.'

'Let's hope it does,' I replied. 'Two thousand pounds takes some finding.'

'I wonder if the national press will write it up,' mused Amy. 'It deserves it. You'll get people from all over the place if it's widely advertised.'

'We've done our best,' I assured her. It's been in all the local papers, I know.'

'I think I shall send a letter to *The Times*,' said Amy, climbing elegantly into her car. 'We want to cast the net *really wide*.'

She drove off and I returned to the school house. Distant voices in the lane and the sound of cars starting on their homeward journeys formed the epilogue to Basil Bradley's moving production.

A star, bright as a jewel, hung beside St Patrick's spire. It looked hopeful, I thought, as I prepared for bed. If the rest of the Fairacre contributions matched this evening's in splendour, our Festival must surely succeed, and more important still, Queen Anne's chalice would remain among those who loved it so well.

CHAPTER SEVEN

Next morning I began to realize just how far-flung the news of our Fairacre Festival had been.

There was a hearty banging on the classroom door during our history lesson and in walked a thickset man wearing a crewcut and a broad smile. The likeness to our Mr Lamb at the Post Office was unmistakable.

'Miss Read?' he began.

'George Lamb,' I said. 'How nice of you to look in!'

'Well, you see, I was raised in this place and I felt I just had to take another peek at this old schoolroom. Don't appear to have changed much since my time. Bit cleaner, perhaps.'

'You'd better repeat that to Mrs Pringle,' I told him. 'It'll make her day.'

I turned to the class.

'Stand up and say "Good-morning" to Mr

Lamb, who was once a pupil here.'

There were welcoming cries and smiles, all the warmer because any interruption to lessons is a pleasurable one.

'That's a Coggs,' exclaimed our visitor, pointing delightedly at Joseph in the front row.

'Quite right,' I said. 'He's Arthur Coggs's son.'

'Oh, I know *Arthur*,' replied George Lamb with some emphasis. I had no doubt that he knew a great deal about his old schoolmate's fondness for liquor and the resultant shindies in our village.

I settled the children to some work and accompanied our guest on a tour of the room.

'Not the same piano! Sakes alive, that must be going on for a century.'

'Eighty, anyway,' I agreed, fingering the walnut fretwork front, and the ivory keys, yellow with age.

'And still the same gaps in the partition,' he went on, bending down to squint through a crack into the infants' room. 'The things we poked through there you'd just never credit, Miss Read.'

'Mr Willet's told me,' I assured him. 'Stinging nettles, knitting needles, dozens of notes—yes, I can well imagine. It happens still, you know. Children don't change much.'

He ambled appreciatively round the room, touching the walls, peering from the windows, and ruffling the children's hair as he passed.

71

'I hear Miss Clare's still at Beech Green. I'm paying her a visit before I fly home.'

'She'll be so pleased,' I said truthfully.

'I owe a lot to her,' he said, suddenly grave. 'Taught us all proper manners and to think for others. She used to say grace before we went home at night. It went: "Bless us this night and make us ever mindful of the wants of others." I always liked that. "Mindful of the wants of others." Good words those.'

He gazed through the window as he spoke, his eyes fixed upon the men working upon St Patrick's belfry.

'They're getting on very well. They've almost finished,' I said, intending to release the tension a little. George Lamb shook himself into the present again.

'Ah! Looks pretty tidy now. You been to the show there yet?'

I said that I had.

'I'm taking some of the chaps who flew over with me tomorrow night. All helps the funds. I owe a lot to Fairacre, and it'll give the fellows no end of a kick to see a building that's over eight hundred years old, and to hear Jean Cole too.'

He glanced at the square gold watch upon his wrist and grimaced.

'Best get back to the Post Office for my lunch, or I'll catch it,' he said. 'Goodbye, Miss Read. Goodbye children. Hope you'll look back on your days at Fairacre School with as

72

much pleasure as I do.'

I accompanied him to the gate. Above the elm trees the rooks were circling high.

'Sign of rain, eh?' he said. ' "Winding up the water," we used to say as kids. You know one thing, Miss Read? Everything seems a lot smaller in Fairacre than I remember it except St Patrick's spire and them old elm trees! Maybe they've both been growing since I left here.'

Chuckling at his own fancies, he made his way back to the village.

*   *   *

On Tuesday evening came the eagerly awaited visit of Jean Cole.

Halfway through the recorded story of Fairacre there was an interval. A spotlight lit the chancel arch and the vicar led in the majestic figure of Major Gunning's cousin. She was resplendent in a long glittering black gown, and her appearance alone was enough to awe her country admirers, but when that glorious voice wrapped us in its warmth and beauty we were touched as never before.

She sang the aria from Handel's *Judas Maccabaeus*, to Mr Annett's accompaniment on the organ. It was a felicitous choice for it celebrated the restoration of the Sanctuary of Jerusalem. We sat in wonderment as the lovely voice soared and fell, and when finally she bowed and left us, we still sat silent and spellbound, whilst through my mind ran Shelley's lines:

> Music, when soft voices die,
> Vibrates in the memory—

I heard later that George Lamb was as good as his word, and that eight of his business friends had been among that evening's congregation.

After the performance was over, it appears, the vicar found them looking round the church in the company of the honorary architect, Mr Graham. He was busy pointing out the particular beauties of the building, and had a fascinated audience. The vicar joined the party and was moved to see the awed admiration with which the strangers viewed the ancient building.

'Back home,' said one, 'we reckon two hundred years as mighty old. It takes your breath away to touch a wall or a doorway this ancient.'

They wandered from vestry to belfry, from altar to sidechapel, and finally emerged from the west door and accepted the vicar's invitation to coffee at the vicarage.

'I can offer you Drambuie with it,' said the vicar with pleasure, as he handed round the steaming cups, 'or a liqueur called aurum, distilled from oranges, and brought from Italy as a present by some friends in the village.'

'Not for me,' said Jock Graham austerely 'but I'll no refuse a good Scots liqueur like Drambuie.'

He was in a remarkably mellow mood. To have such an attentive audience was a joy to him. The villagers of Fairacre took their church very much for granted, but these strangers were perceptive and appreciative. Jock Graham's tongue wagged all the faster, as the Drambuie diminished sip by sip, and he extolled the unique attributes of the building he loved so well.

It was almost half-past eleven when at last the party broke up.

'I'd no idea it was so late,' said the vicar. 'Have you far to go?'

'We're booked in at Caxley,' said one. 'Two of us have business there tomorrow. The others are off to London on the early train, rustling up some more customers we hope.'

Farewells were made, and the vicar and Mrs Partridge turned back into the hall.

'What very nice fellows!' exclaimed Mr Partridge. 'George Lamb seems to have found some good companions.'

'And a wife who's interested in cooking,' added Mrs Partridge. 'He's going to ask her to send me a recipe for almond cookies.'

'Cookies?' repeated the vicar, his brow furrowed with perplexity.

'*Cookies!*' said his wife firmly. 'Biscuits to us.

Really, Gerald, at times you are hopelessly insular.'

'I suppose so,' agreed the vicar rather sadly. Then his face brightened.

'But we've broadened our horizons tonight, my dear, haven't we? With our American friends, and prima donnas!'

Amicably, they mounted the stairs to bed.

*   *   *

The day came when Fairacre School presented its contribution to the Festival. We had decided to give two performances, one in the afternoon when mothers with young children could come, and one in the evening when fathers could attend.

We chose Wednesday for the simple reason that it is early closing day in Caxley and that the people of Fairacre would not be tempted to go there to spend their money. Thursday is market day, and three buses run from our village into Caxley on that busy day. We could not hope to compete with Caxley's magnetic pull on a Thursday. Besides, as Mrs Bonny pointed out reasonably, they would have more money to put in the silver collection *before* market day.

Excitement had mounted steadily during the Festival week and by the time Wednesday came it was at fever-pitch. The costumes and simple properties had been stacked on desks at

76

the side of my room and Mrs Bonny's, for want of any other place to put them, and mighty little work had been done by the children with such attractions lying near by. Pens in hand, arithmetic exercises neglected before them, the children's bemused gaze turned constantly to the glamorous heaps of clothes. Here was a glimpse of another world. Our country children rarely go to the theatre. An annual visit to the pantomime is about all that comes their way. Here, close at hand, were all the trappings of magic, the means of slipping from the everyday world of school to one of enchanting fantasy. It was little wonder that I had very few sums to mark each day. But a wise teacher knows when she is beaten, and I forbore to scold.

As soon as school dinner was demolished we set about arranging the seating. The partition was pushed back, the desks removed either to the playground or to one end to form the basis of the stage. Mr Willet, Mr Roberts the farmer, and Jim Farrow his shepherd, arranged the long planks across the desks, tried the curtains we had rigged up, and pronounced the stage ready.

Meanwhile, the children were putting the chairs in rows for the audience. These were new stackable beauties from the village hall, and we had been threatened with all sorts of penalties if any damage were done.

The din was appalling. The metal frames of the chairs clanged like an iron foundry. The men's voices, raised above the racket, were thunderous. The thud of their mallets as they knocked the planks into place reverberated among the pitch-pine rafters above. When at last the work was done, and the men had departed, Mrs Bonny and I took an aspirin and a cup of tea apiece in the hope of curing our headaches.

At two-thirty the schoolroom was packed tight. In the front seats were the vicar and the managers and a number of illustrious friends of the school. Parents, aunts and uncles, little brothers and sisters and numerous distant relations, whom I had never seen before, kept up a cheerful hum of conversation while panic grew steadily behind the stage curtain.

The first item was a collection of folksongs sung by the whole school. It was a tight squash to get all sixty-odd children on to the stage, and one scaremonger among the infants told everyone that 'them planks ain't safe', thus causing widespread terror.

'Anyone who wants to get off the stage can do so,' I said fiercely. 'But don't forget your mothers have come to see you.'

This quelled the riot a trifle, but Mrs Bonny and I had the usual fears to calm.

'S'pose us forgets the words?'

'S'pose there's a fire. Which door does we go for?'

'I feels a bit sick.'

'I forgets how the tune goes.'

'John Todd shoved me!'

'I never then!'

'Miss, there ain't enough room for us up this end. The wall's all coming off on my sleeve, miss. My *best* sleeve.'

At this moment, Mrs Bonny was obliged to take three of her youngest to the lavatory—an inevitable hold-up at any school function— whilst I applied my eye to the crack of the curtain to watch the audience. It really was a wonderful house, kindly and enthusiastic, and I only hoped we should not disappoint all those present.

At last all was ready. Mrs Bonny took her seat at the piano. United in the face of their common ordeal, the children grew suddenly silent. I hauled on the curtain rope, and we were off to a flying start.

*   *   *

The deafening applause which greeted every item was most gratifying. The infants, naturally, won the palm, and every time the curtain rose upon them there were loving cries of: 'Oh, aren't they sweet?' 'Look at our Billy!' 'The pretty dears!' 'Don't they sing lovely?' and the like. They certainly went through their paces magnificently, after initial bashfulness, and the folk dance nearly brought the roof— and the stage—down with energetic clapping and stamping.

79

This number ended the first half and we could hear the infants hard at it as my class prepared for *The Princess and the Swineherd* in the lobby. Ernest, usually so stolid, had become hilariously excited and was clowning about in his finery, reducing the girls to a state of helpless giggling.

The princess's skirt had been trodden on, and given way drastically at the gathers, so that I was obliged to do last-minute repairs with safety pins, with my hand inside her waist-band.

'Oh, miss, you tickles!' giggled Elizabeth, wriggling about like an eel. 'Oh, miss, your hands is cold!' Then a squeal.

'Oh, miss, you've bin and *pricked* me!'

'Stand still then,' I begged, snapping the last pin home. 'There, now you'll do!'

'It's pinned to my vest, miss.'

'And that's how it will have to stay,' I assured her flatly. 'We're on in five minutes.'

These words had a dual effect. Some children were, mercifully, struck dumb. Others became panic-stricken and fussed even more vociferously. Luckily, applause and cheers broke out from the schoolroom at this stage, the infants came trooping back, flushed with success, and we were obliged to collect our senses ready for our big moment after the brief interval.

'The magic saucepan's bin and gone!' exclaimed Patrick dramatically. This was the highly necessary property round which the

Princess and her ladies gathered to discover the meals being cooked all over the town. There was a frenzied scattering of costumes, searching under chairs and general confusion until one of the infants, flown with success, was discovered with it on his head from whence it was wrenched by one of his enraged elders.

'You might have had his ears off,' observed an onlooker dispassionately, but relief was so general that no one took much notice of this true statement.

After all the excitement I was prepared to find the cast both agitated and wordless, but all went well. Ernest's courtly bows were marvels of grace, and the only slight slip was the addition of 's' now and again, in true Fairacre fashion.

'We knows who's going to have sweet soup and pancakes! We knows who's going to have porridge and chops!' chanted the ladies exultantly. At least, I told myself philosophically, they did not say 'Us knows', as they might so easily have done.

The applause at the end of the performance was deafening, and augured well for the repeat programme in the evening.

By the time the children and their parents had gone home, Mrs Bonny and I were dog tired. We tottered across to my house, and revived our strength with tea, tomato sandwiches and shortbread.

'Mr Willet says we've taken over seven

pounds this afternoon, and it should be as much again this evening,' said Mrs Bonny, surveying her stockinged feet at the other end of the sofa. 'It should help the funds quite a lot.'

'It should,' I agreed. We lapsed into exhausted silence, and I guessed that her thoughts were running on the same lines as mine. Should we ever, in this small village, even with the herculean efforts we were making, ever come anywhere near the target we had so hopefully and bravely set ourselves?

Three hours later, much refreshed, we crossed the playground for our second house. Against a ravishing blue sky, the newly gilded weathercock flamed triumphantly on the pinnacle of St Patrick's spire. It was a heartening sight.

Resolutely we thrust our doubts from us, pushed open the heavy school door, and were engulfed once again by our teeming mob.

CHAPTER EIGHT

Our School Concert, which finally netted sixteen pounds for the funds, was one of the more modest efforts in Festival Week. It was on a par with the Mammoth Whist Drive, the Giant Draw and the Fabulous Flower Show. The *Son et Lumière*, with the added attraction

82

of Jean Cole, was the backbone of the week, of course, and was so successful that it was decided to carry on for the next week as well, much to everyone's joy.

It was fortunate that it had done so well, for calamity hit Fairacre the day before the fête. Peter Martin, whose advent we had all awaited so eagerly, was involved in a car crash on Thursday evening, and was taken to hospital with two broken ribs and concussion.

We heard the news on radio and television that evening and were plunged into gloom. The vicar, good Christian that he is, forbore to express what was in most of our minds, simply saying: 'Poor young fellow!! It is a mercy that his injuries are no worse!'

Jock Graham was more outspoken.

'This'll make a difference to the takings,' he observed dourly, reading the headlines in Friday's *Guardian*.

'He won't die, will he, miss?' asked a bevy of little girls round my desk. Peter Martin's injuries and the cruelty of Fate in thus snatching him from us were the playground topics of the day, and in fact, of the whole neighbourhood.

Lady Sawston, who lives locally, nobly agreed to step into the breach and to open the fête, but it was quite apparent that fewer people would attend now that our star attraction had gone.

It was a sore blow indeed to our efforts.

But the final item in the Festival's programme was the Gala Dance which was held in the Village Hall on Saturday evening and at which Peter Martin was to have sung. It was the culmination of our efforts, and the ladies of the Floral Society excelled themselves with shower arrangements on every wall bracket and a bank of massed flowers, contributed from Fairacre cottage gardens, across the width of the stage.

Homemade refreshments had been billed as one of the chief attractions, my own modest contribution consisting of two dozen sausage rolls and a rather handsome set of small savouries in aspic jelly, so ravishingly pretty—at least, in my own eyes—that I hoped that Amy might drop in unexpectedly and be impressed. Needless to say, she did not, and the only comment which I heard on their appearance came from Mrs Mawne, who remarked disparagingly to one of her helpers: 'Probably sent by the vicar's wife. She dabbles in aspic.' *Dabbles in aspic indeed*, I thought, smarting in silence. It is hardly surprising that Mrs Mawne is so generally detested.

I looked in during the last hour of the event. Faces were flushed, skirts whirling, you could have cut the air with a knife, and 'The Dizzy Beat' from Caxley lived up to its name, with enough tympani to drown the other three instruments.

It was a huge success, and I joined with zest

the great circle for 'Auld Lang Syne', and wrenched other people's arms from their sockets with enthusiasm matching my neighbour's. After 'God Save The Queen', the company drifted away to the sound of car engines, roaring motor bikes and farewell cries, and I helped to wash up the debris.

Mrs Willet accompanied me home. It was lovely to be out in the cool night air. Someone had night-scented stocks growing in his front garden, and the fragrance was delicious. A half-moon lay on its back, cradled in the tree-tops, and an owl hooted from the vicarage cedar tree.

'A beautiful night,' said Mrs Willet. 'And a successful one. Do you think the vicar will know the result of the Festival Week tomorrow? Everyone's praying we'll have made enough to save the chalice, though they don't say much.'

'We'll live in hope,' I replied, opening my gate. 'We couldn't have done more anyway. That's one comfort.'

*   *   *

The vicar did not make an announcement the next day, but the hand on the Appeal's board shot round to one thousand and seven hundred pounds.

'Getting along now!' said the parishioners excitedly, as they made their way past the board. 'It's coming on, isn't it?'

'But not fast enough,' was Mr Mawne's comment to the vicar, after the service.

'I agree with you there,' said Jock Graham soberly. 'I've kept a tight eye on the money all the way along the line, and give Christie's their due, they've done a fine job at a reasonable price.'

'What is still outstanding?' inquired the vicar, leading the two to the vicarage for a glass of sherry.

'My estimate, a generous one, was two thousand. Christie's have had two lots of four hundred so far, the rest to be paid when the job is finished. That's twelve hundred to find. With luck we'll find the total is something under two thousand, and the rest can go into the Fabric Fund. We must have something behind us in case of further disaster.'

'God forbid!' exclaimed the vicar, his mouth working piteously. He poured a sherry with a shaking hand, and they sipped in silence. Mr Mawne broke it at last.

It's no good, Gerald. You must go into this business of the sale of the chalice. It's all very well to be sentimental—'

'*Sentimental!*' cried the vicar, but his friend swept on.

'But the fact is that the chalice could be our salvation. Not only now, but as a hedge against future crises. After all, we could always have a replica made.'

86

'*A replica?*' echoed the vicar in anguish. 'But it wouldn't be the same!'

'Of course not,' agreed Mr Mawne soothingly, as if addressing a fractious child, 'but it would do as well.'

The vicar, too stunned to explain, shook his grey head sadly. Jock Graham, unusually perceptive, spoke gently.

'It's a sore blow, I know, vicar, but it would be prudent to find out the possibilities. With any luck, it may never be needed, but it's only fair that the parish should know the position. We need another five or six hundred pounds to pay for this damage and to put the Fabric Fund on a sound footing. The Festival may bring in another sixty to seventy. There are the sums from the guarantors and the covenantors which will bring in another hundred or so, over a period of time. But it just isn't enough.'

The vicar put down his sherry glass carefully and looked from one to the other.

'Let me sleep on it,' he said. 'I'll give you an answer, one way or the other, early next week. It's a step I can hardly bear to contemplate.'

'Good man!' said Mr Mawne encouragingly, slapping his old friend painfully on the back, and the two men left the vicar to his own troubled thoughts.

'Simply pecking at your food, Gerald,' commented his wife, briskly removing the plates at lunch-time. 'You worry far too much. You'll have another of your dizzy spells, if

87

you're not sensible.'

'I'll have a walk this afternoon,' said the vicar meekly. 'Fresh air always calms me.'

The road to the downs above Fairacre peters out into a grassy track. Birds darted across the vicar's path, with cries of alarm. Rabbits bounded away with a flourish of white scuts, and at least four larks vied with each other high against the blue and white dappled sky. It looked so peaceful, so unchanging, much as it looked, thought the vicar, with a pang, when the silversmith had finished his masterpiece, in the reign of Queen Anne, over two hundred and fifty years ago.

He sat himself heavily on the springy turf and plucked a nearby harebell, twisting its wiry stem this way and that as he gazed at the village spread out below.

What should he do? He had had faith that his prayers would be answered, but God in His wisdom had seemed to withhold the easy way. There, below him, the villagers rested after their wholehearted efforts in Festival Week. The response had been wonderful, the village united as never before. There could be very little more expected from them. Henry Mawne was right. More help must come from another source, and the only possibility was the chalice. He must bring himself to approach the Bishop and to seek his advice. He owed it to his church and to his villagers. He had been selfish and weak in refusing to face the facts.

He sighed heavily, and the view below him grew suddenly blurred. Sad at heart, he struggled to his feet and made his way home.

*   *   *

The vicar slept little in the nights that followed. He had met Mr Mawne and Jock Graham and agreed reluctantly to consult the Bishop. It had taken him a week to compose a letter, and now he awaited a reply in an agony of spirit.

One morning he sat leaden-eyed before his breakfast egg, surveying the pile of letters. There was no word yet from the Bishop, but among the bills, receipts and circulars was a long blue air mail envelope, as gaudy as a peacock among sparrows. The vicar took it up first, savouring this rare foreign treasure.

'George Washington had a fine face,' he observed, studying the stamps closely. 'And what a good idea these little address tickets are! So much more legible than some unknown hand-writing at the head of a letter.'

'Who's it from?' asked Mrs Partridge, cutting to the heart of the matter.

'Oh, now let me see. "G. D. Lamb," it says. Lamb,' said the vicar ruminatively. 'Do we know a Mr Lamb in America, my dear?'

'Of course we do,' exclaimed his wife impatiently. 'George Lamb who was here during the Festival. That's probably the recipe for almond cookies he promised me. Do open it, dear, and *please* eat your breakfast. I want to clear the table. I'm having a coffee morning here today to raise more funds.'

The vicar obediently took a bite of toast and then slit the envelope. The letter was written in a firm hand in good copperplate which owed its beginnings to Miss Clare's guidance, many years earlier.

Mrs Partridge watched her husband's eyes widen and his face grow pinker as he perused the paper in his hand. At last, bemused, he put it down, and rummaging in the envelope produced a cheque which he studied with stupefaction.

'Is my recipe there?' asked Mrs Partridge. The vicar shook his head slowly, as if to clear it, rather than in answer to his wife's query. He seemed beyond speech.

'Has he sent something to the Fund?' asked Mrs Partridge, her glance falling on the cheque. 'How very, very kind of him!'

The vicar opened his mouth, and shut it again. He took a sip of coffee, and then found his voice.

'He has sent us a cheque for two thousand dollars.'

'*No!*' said his wife, thunderstruck. He *can't* have done! Not even Americans are as rich as that, and George only has a catering business which he built up himself!'

Without a word, the vicar handed the

cheque across the table.

'It must be two thousand, because it's got it in words as well as figures,' said Mrs Partridge, studying the cheque earnestly, and speaking with great care as though she were explaining matters to herself. 'I simply can't take this in, Gerald.'

'It's not George alone, my dear. It appears that his good friends on the trip were most concerned to hear of our plight, and contributed very generously, and also got other people to do so. George says in his letter that two old ladies, whose parents came from these parts originally, gave a considerable part of the money, and so did some relatives of George's wife. Can you believe it, my dear? We have been wonderfully blest.'

'It is absolutely wonderful!' said his wife huskily. 'In the face of such generosity one hardly knows whether to laugh or cry. Oh, Gerald, this will save the chalice, won't it?'

'It was my first thought,' confessed the vicar. 'I must telephone Henry immediately, and Jock, and then we must get in touch with the Rural Dean and the Bishop.'

He pushed back his chair and came round the table to kiss his wife. He looked, she thought, as though twenty years had fallen from him in the last five minutes.

She watched him affectionately as he gazed once again at the cheque.

'How does one translate it into pounds?' he

asked.

'Divide by three,' said Mrs Partridge promptly. 'That's somewhere near. Henry will know exactly.'

'But that means this is worth almost seven hundred pounds! It is quite incredible! To think that people who have never seen us or our little church should be so overwhelmingly generous! It does one's heart good.'

'The same sort of thing happened at Dorchester Abbey,' his wife reminded him. 'And there was a simply lovely service of thanksgiving with lots of Americans there. Remember?'

'Yes, indeed,' nodded the vicar. 'And there will be one here in Fairacre before very long, I can promise you.'

He picked up George Lamb's letter and put it carefully, with the cheque, into his wallet.

'I shall do my telephoning, and write this morning to George and all his kind friends,' he said. 'But what I shall say, I really don't know. My heart is too full.'

The joyous news flashed round the Fairacre grapevine within hours, helped considerably by the partakers of coffee at Mrs Partridge's morning meeting. Villagers were incredulous at first, and then genuinely touched by the unexpected benefaction. Even Mrs Pringle seemed moved by the magnificence of the present, though she was grudging in her first pronouncements to me.

'That George Lamb must've done well for himself in New York. Been fleecing the customers, I shouldn't wonder.'

I was roused to wrath and told her that the idea may certainly have been George's, but the bulk of the money was from Americans who had never even seen St Patrick's, which made the gesture even more wonderful. Mrs Pringle had the grace to look a little sheepish as she spread a tea towel over the hot boiler to dry.

'Yes, that's true,' she conceded. 'I've always understood the Americans—for all their funny ways—had a feeling heart. And say what you like, Miss Read, it's a feeling heart that matters when you're in trouble. They tell me the vicar's already planning a thanksgiving service as soon as the repairs is done.'

'We'll all be there,' I promised her.

EPILOGUE

Exactly a year after the fateful night which wrecked the roof of St Patrick's, the bells were rehung in the repaired belfry.

Now all was completed. The spire and the roof presented their usual tidy aspect to the village. At last the scaffolding had gone. The workmen's huts had vanished, and the trodden grass of the churchyard was fast returning to its velvety greenness under Mr Willet's tending. The hand on the Appeal Fund board stood triumphantly at well over two thousand pounds thanks to the efforts of the folk of Fairacre and their friends near and far.

In his study, the vicar was composing the sermon he would be giving the next Sunday at the great thanksgiving service. On his desk stood Queen Anne's silver chalice reflecting the autumn sunshine in its mellow curves. The vicar touched its ancient beauty with loving fingers. In a few minutes it would be in the kitchen being cleaned by Mrs Partridge in readiness for its part in the festivities of the great day.

What hopes and fears had centred round this lovely thing during the past year, he thought! What a year it had been for them all in Fairacre!

He pushed aside his papers and went into

the garden for a breath of air. It was a quiet, gentle day with no breath of wind, a contrast indeed with the fury of the first of October last year when disaster had struck.

He thought with gratitude of all the blessings which had followed—the united efforts of all in the village, the bravery, the generosity of everybody, particularly of those American friends who had forged an unforgettable link with this small unknown village, as a result of last year's storm. What friends Fairacre had made! What fun it had been!

He stooped to pick up a shred of paper which was lodged among the button chrysanthemums in the border. He smoothed it out and surveyed the lettering with a smile of intense happiness. Crumpled, rain-washed and faded, it was the final triumphant scrap of

The Fairacre Festival

TIGGY

CONTENTS

To
Gwen and Edith
who first befriended
Tiggy

CHAPTER ONE

THE LAST CAT

It all began during one of those long hot summers which are so rare in England.

The winter had been dreary and protracted, with the usual flurries of snow, slippery roads, fog and rain. But there had been nothing dramatic about it—no ten-foot drifts of snow to cut us off from the market town, no spectacular hard frosts forming a fringe of icicles along the thatched roofs. What we had endured was simply tedious coldness, dark mornings, and a remarkable dearth of winter sunlight.

We longed for the Spring, and it took its time in coming that year. The daffodils and narcissi in the garden poked their green shoots through the soil, but refused to grow further in the coldness. The buds of the flowering currant—usually some of the earliest to break out in cheering fan-like leaf—remained sealed, and the bare winter tracery of the trees continued in its nakedness until well on into March.

It must have been in that month that I woke one night to hear the caterwauling of love-sick cats. Certainly, it was very cold as I shivered in my nightgown looking out of the bedroom window. Two black shapes raced squawking across the garden and disappeared from view, and I returned to bed again, remembering Timmy.

There has been a cat in the house for many, many years. Paddy was followed by Tinker when she died at fifteen years of age. Tinker, a noble tabby of great sagacity and bravery, lived until he was almost twenty.

It was not easy to replace such a lovable old warrior, but I had promised a young girl 'to save from the bucket' one of the many kittens born at her parents' farm in Oxfordshire.

'But it must be a tom-cat,' I stipulated. We had had a hair-raising experience, years before, with a spayed female, and I felt that I could face only a simple neutering operation.

We collected Timmy in the late summer. He was the only male, and pathetically frightened. His sisters were bonny fat lumps, and the farmer was most anxious for us to have one of these stronger specimens.

'We usually have much better kittens than that,' he told me, surveying the black and white scrap in the cat basket. But I was confident that Timmy would thrive, and we bore him home.

His first terrified dash, when he was released in the kitchen, was to sanctuary behind the refrigerator. With appalling difficulty he was rescued from the machinery underneath, and left with a warm blanket, an earth tray, minced meat and milk.

Not a sound was heard during the night, and next morning the meat and milk had gone.

At the sight of a human being, however, he fled underneath the dresser, and virtually made his home there for three weeks. Fortunately, he cottoned on to the use of the earth tray, and emerged for this important function. But food and drink had to be put by the dresser, and he rarely approached it while people were about.

Time passed. He grew braver, and eventually discovered the garden, and liked to play and hide in a tall old hedge. Luckily, he seemed to ignore the road which runs by the cottage. Although, on the map, this is an unclassified road, it carries a considerable amount of heavy traffic, and we knew the risk we were running when Timmy was adopted.

Before long the inevitable happened. One back leg was broken, presumably by a glancing blow from a vehicle. For six weeks, the poor kitten's leg was in plaster and strapped up to his chest while the bone knitted together, and for this period he was naturally immobile.

He became increasingly dear during these weeks. He had two cries. One for liver, which constituted the major part of his diet, and one for his earth tray. It was easy enough to push a saucer under his chin at meal-times, but not so easy to support him over his earth tray, but it had to be done, and amazing though it may seem, there was never an accident throughout his period of immobility.

It was a great day when he was free from the plaster, and he could potter around the garden again. His distrust of the road was heartening. Now he turned left automatically from the cat-flap on the back door. It seemed as though Timmy could look forward to a ripe old age.

But it was not to be. A few months later, still weak no doubt, he picked up an infection, and died within a few days.

It was heart-breaking. He had had such a sad, brief life. We felt, somehow, that we had let him down, despite all our efforts.

'That's it!' we told each other, much shaken. 'Never again! It's simply not fair to bring a cat here while the traffic is so heavy. We must face the fact that *we can't have a cat*.'

And having sadly, but very sensibly, made our decision we settled down to being cat-less.

*   *   *

It was perfectly horrible.

The house seemed dead. There was no greeting when one returned home, no milk bowl on the kitchen floor, no cat-made dent in the eiderdown.

Little kitchen tit-bits such as bacon rinds, giblets or fish skin, once put aside on old saucers for luscious cat-snacks, were now put out for the birds.

Friends were constantly offering kittens, each more adorable than the last. Heart-rending tales of unwanted, homeless, mis-used cats had to be met with unnatural stoniness.

'That awful road!' we said.

'Certain death!' we said.

'Not fair to a cat!' we said.

'Never again!' we said.

We were wonderfully sure of ourselves.

CHAPTER TWO

DROUGHT

The long cold months were bleaker than ever without a cat, but at last they passed.

The cottage garden suddenly burst into life, fragrant with the heady scent of narcissi and daffodils.

The sun shone steadily. As the early spring bulbs faded, the lilac and laburnum brought their splendour, and the copper beech and ancient apple tree added to the gaiety.

We all revelled in the sunshine. This is downland chalky country, but a cap of heavy clay, some hundreds of acres in extent, covers the chalk hereabouts. Our little hamlet is situated upon this clay cap.

Our heavy soil is difficult to work, cold and glutinous in wet weather. Gardeners reckon that crops here are three or four weeks behind the valley crops, for we are high too, and open to the winds.

But, of course, we score when there is a hot spell, for the heavy soil retains the moisture. When plants in the chalky gardens are drooping, ours are still thriving. And our roses take a lot of beating, for they relish the clay.

So, for many weeks, we enjoyed the dry weather, never doubting that rain would come before the gardens began to suffer.

But very little came. By July the clay was hard, and cracks had appeared in the borders and lawns. The bird bath was filled twice a day, and provided refreshment, not only for sparrows, finches, blackbirds, thrushes, robins and all the other friendly birds, but also for the bees which clung to the rim of the water, drinking thirstily.

It is a cruelly dry area in a drought. Older people in the village remember that a horse and cart spent the day going up and down the steep hill from the River Lambourn, some two miles away, fetching water for villagers, sheep, cattle, and the many farm horses. It was a great day when a deep bore was sunk in one of the gardens, and the inhabitants could fetch buckets of cold pure water from the chalk far below.

In the field opposite the cottage, the cows grazed. A galvanised water trough stood in one corner, beneath the trees, and I noticed that it leaked. A large shallow puddle formed beside it, and this was the meeting place of the more timid birds, such as rooks and lapwings. Many a small animal, that hot summer, must have found refreshment there.

As the hot weather continued, I took to putting out a shallow bowl of water near the bird bath, and soon discovered that a hedgehog—perhaps more than one—visited it at night.

I am particularly fond of these nice little snuffling creatures and each night put out an old enamel plate, once the redoubtable Tinker's dinner dish, with bread and milk upon it.

First I soaked the bread well in warm water, squeezed it out, and then poured over a little milk. This rather Spartan fare appeared to be relished by the hedgehog, for every morning I collected an empty plate from the lawn, with growing elation.

'Look!' I'd say proudly. 'The hedgehogs have eaten the lot!'

'More likely a ghastly great rat,' was the comment one morning.

'Probably the birds,' said a neighbour. 'Have you actually *seen* the hedgehog?'

I had to admit that I had not. But there were certainly plenty of hedgehog droppings about, and I was confident that a Mrs Tiggywinkle, and relatives too, probably, enjoyed my parsimonious bounty. Later, I was to suffer pangs of remorse at the thought of that watery bread, so frugally sprinkled with milk.

One evening, about the end of July, my neighbour took her black Labrador dog for his usual evening walk. She crossed the road, and strolled down the edge of the field where the cattle trough stood. A row of fine old trees divides this field from the next, and beneath them runs some leafy undergrowth composed of various bushes, such as elder and blackberry interspersed with bracken, some dozen or so yards in width.

About half-way down, Nick the Labrador, stopped to investigate the undergrowth. This was a spot about a hundred yards from the road.

A fierce hissing and spitting came from the bushes, and Nick was called to heel. He obeyed, but a few evenings later when he was taken that way again, he repeated his visit, only to be greeted with the same response. We know now that a cat with newly-born kittens was hidden there.

*　　　*　　　*

My cottage is one of three, each set in a roomy garden well furnished with trees and shrubs. Between the three of us we must harbour scores of birds' nests in our thick hedges, and certainly plenty of moles, voles and field mice which live in the soil beneath their shade.

The third cottage is not occupied continuously, but the owner is a keen fisherman and is there always during the trout fishing season and often at other times of the year. He is looked after by two maids—friends for many years—whose kitchen window overlooks the road and has a view of the row of trees where Nick had encountered the hidden source of the mysterious hissing.

On several occasions, about this time, they came down in the morning to find that the lid of the dustbin had been knocked off. The remains of meat-stained paper, well-chewed, were about, and it was plain that some desperately hungry animal was raiding the bin for any scraps, however unappetizing.

One morning, they saw a small black cat, with white feet, moving about under the cover of the hedge. She was pathetically thin and dusty, and her interest in the dustbin proved that she was the nightly marauder.

The kindly friends moved towards her to stroke her, but she backed away nervously. Obviously, she didn't trust human beings.

They filled a saucer with milk and put it outside in the shade. They closed the door and watched from inside. Very soon, the cat appeared, and though nervous and anxiously alert, she lapped ravenously. It was quite apparent that she was almost starving.

Milk and food were put out regularly, and

the cat became less timid. She let the friends approach her, and they saw that she was a mother cat, who had recently had kittens, and must be feeding a family somewhere nearby.

Two or three evenings later they were lucky enough to see the family at play. It was an enchanting sight. There appeared to be five or six kittens, tabby, black, ginger—all tumbling about, sparring with each other, or making their wobbly way, small triangular tails erect, to suck milk from their mother who lay near them in the evening sunshine, watching their antics indulgently.

But the friends' delight in this pretty sight was mixed with anxiety. The family's hideaway was across the road—that road along which traffic pounded night and day. The mother must already cross it several times daily to eat and drink the good things put out at the back door.

How soon would it be before the kittens too discovered the saucers of food and followed their mother into danger?

It seemed that the mother cat's life, and that of her babies, had been saved by the kindness of the two friends. But what of the future? If only she had found a home for them on the right side of that wretched road, they told each other anxiously.

They need not have worried.

The cat had summed up the situation perfectly.

CHAPTER THREE

MRS TIGGYWINKLE

Of course, we were all interested in the newcomers. I was never lucky enough to see the kittens at this stage, but Nick's mistress confirmed that the new home was some distance from their earlier one, which had been a hundred yards or so further down the hedge.

The present abode was strategically placed, from the cat's point of view. It was much nearer the source of food, a mere twenty yards or so from the bountiful back door. Moreover, it was very close indeed to the leaking cattle trough, and the large shallow puddle at which the mother cat could teach the kittens to lap. It must have been a godsend to them in that blazing summer.

Tall dry grass and thick undergrowth hid the babies from sight. She had provided for them beautifully, and she ruled them so strictly, it became clear, that they were trained to stay under cover while she made her forays for food. Many a human parent could have profited by her example. She loved them well enough, but they must do as they were told, for their own safety.

She now began to visit my garden, and I fed

her regularly. Here, I realised, was my hedgehog, my Mrs Tiggywinkle. Watching the poor little cat wolf down scraps, I thought remorsefully of that unpalatable moistened bread which she had been so pleased to devour.

She would not let me touch her, but purred as she ate, and seemed affectionate. By this time, she had grown brave enough to enter the friends' kitchen and let them pet her.

'She's obviously used to a house,' they told me. 'She likes to be inside, and "plucks cotton" on the rug and purrs all the time.'

A few days later they discovered that the whole family had been brought across the road during the night, and were in their third home, hidden in the bushes near the back door, handy for the largesse.

Our admiration for this determined little cat grew as we thought about the planning and the work which had gone into all her manoeuvres.

This latest move had obviously been the most difficult one.

The shift from the place of birth to the site near the water trough must have posed some problems, but it did not involve crossing the busy road. The kittens too, may have been small enough to be carried in her mouth to the second place. Nevertheless, they had to be carried one at a time, and meanwhile the others had been made to realise that they must stay put until fetched.

By the time the move across the road came, the kittens were too big to be carried. She must have shepherded them one at a time, when there were lulls in the flow of traffic, and made sure that the kittens on each side of the road remained where they were told to remain. It probably took her all night to complete the operation. Later events support this supposition, as you shall hear.

Most of the time the kittens stayed hidden, but the two friends saw enough to realise that there were six altogether.

'Perhaps seven,' they said. 'There's one much larger than the others—rather ugly, and a brownish colour. The mother cat doesn't seem to like it.'

We are fairly sure that this odd man out was one of an earlier litter, who had hung about in the neighbourhood, and was now hoping to attach himself to the new family and benefit from the food supplied from the cottages. The mother cat resented this and did her best to drive him away. No doubt she felt that it was time he fended for himself.

It so happened, that some weeks later I saw a fine tom cat, with brindled fur like a hare's, climbing the lilac tree in my garden. It was intent on dislodging a lump of fat which I had hung there for the tits. It was, I decided, the odd man out, but later events gave me doubts, as you shall hear.

Meanwhile, talking among ourselves, we

pieced together what we knew of the black and white mother cat. She must have been living wild in the area for about eighteen months or two years, we reckoned, and had had one, or possibly two, earlier litters. Several cats had been sighted in the woods nearby and the hedges, and these might have been her descendants.

One mystery was certainly cleared up for me. Timmy had been much the same in looks—black with white feet. My neighbour told me that she had seen him sitting in our porch while we were out one day, but I knew this could not be so, because Timmy was still too frightened to emerge from the house at that time. Obviously, this little stray cat had sat there, and been seen.

It explained too the strange cat whom we had seen dash away from the porch on several occasions when we returned home at night. I think, now, that it was not only shelter she sought, but the proximity of human beings, nervous though she was at our approach. This cat, I feel sure, was once someone's pet.

I remembered too, seeing this same cat leap up the grassy bank bordering the road. The car's headlights had turned her eyes to green fire, and her white feet made her even more conspicuous in the winter darkness.

Yes, it was quite plain that she had been in the neighbourhood for some time, fending for herself and her kittens, and coping with the dangers, not only of the road, but of other more powerful predators than herself, such as foxes.

She visited me regularly now for food, and occasionally let me stroke her while she was feeding. Her coat, once so dirty and rough, began to grow glossy again, her eyes brighter, her purr louder.

I was becoming very fond of her, and my respect for her as a mother grew daily. Nevertheless, I did not want the responsibility of owning her, nor the kittens I had never yet seen.

'I shan't let her indoors,' I said firmly. 'She can have her food regularly, and she can have a bed in the workshop for the winter, if she's still around then, but I'm not having her as an indoor pet. Think of all those kittens to come!'

'It's not fair to take on a cat here,' we said again.

'Not with that awful road,' we said.

'We learned our lesson with poor Timmy,' we said.

But we were, perhaps, a little less sure of ourselves.

'She's a fine little cat,' we agreed, watching her demolish her plateful of food.

'And quite able to look after herself, in the normal way,' we said, throwing a sop to our consciences. 'She probably wouldn't want to stay with us anyway.'

We watched her lick the empty plate, her

eyes half-closed in bliss.

'Even if we could keep her,' we added. 'Which we can't, of course. Quite out of the question.'

Which only goes to show that you should never tempt Providence.

CHAPTER FOUR

THE FAMILY MOVES IN

Two or three weeks passed. The weather remained hot and dry. The farmers were beginning to grumble at the lack of rain, gardeners were forbidden to use sprinklers on their parched lawns, and everyone's waterbutt was empty.

The time came for the fisherman at the third cottage to return to his home. The two maids would be returning too, and they were worried about the cat family who would look in vain for the food and drink which they had supplied so generously.

As the mother cat was coming regularly to me, I promised to continue to put out enough food and drink for all, and so they returned home with easier minds.

But, of course, with the house shut up, it was quite clear that the cat would make another move. Where would she go this time, we wondered?

Although no one saw the move, she evidently returned across the road to the second home in the undergrowth, near the water trough. It still leaked, and a generous puddle gave the young family drinking water.

The mother continued to come daily for her food, but I still saw no sign of the kittens, although I walked across the road and peered several times among the bushes. Not so much as a squeak or rustle betrayed their presence. They had been well-disciplined, and warned against dangerous human beings.

One morning, about a week after the friends had returned home, Nick's mistress told me of the night's adventures.

'The mother cat brought them across the road,' she said, 'one after the other, at about half-hourly intervals.' The night had been light, and she had watched the operation with enormous interest.

'The last kitten was tiresome and ran away up the road, but the mother sprinted after it, and headed it back.'

'And where did she take them?' I asked. I had a horrid feeling that I knew the answer already.

'I *think*,' said my neighbour, 'I *rather think* that she's put them all in your log shed!'

'Oh, no!' I cried in dismay. But at the same time I felt laughter bubbling inside. Trust a cat! Wasn't I the perfect person to land a cat family on? My neighbour already had a handsome ginger cat Topper, and Nick the Labrador. My house was empty of animals, and food had been supplied regularly. Moreover, the log shed offered warmth, shelter and a perfect hiding place for the kittens. With her usual sagacity, the cat had put her plan into action.

And, it seemed, it had succeeded.

*   *   *

Or had it?

During the next two or three days, work went on by the open-ended log shed. We were putting down some paving stones at its entrance, and the noise and activity were considerable. Not once were the kittens in evidence. Not a whisker, not a tail, not a mew, not a hiss. Nothing.

'They *can't* be there,' I said. 'They wouldn't stay hidden for that length of time. Anyway we should have seen the mother lurking around. She must have taken them somewhere else. Perhaps into our hedge. They're certainly not in those logs.'

Still the cat appeared for her meals, but where from, and where she went when they were demolished, I had no idea.

On the following Saturday I went to a fête. The weather was still glorious, and I returned in the golden evening well-content with the fun I had enjoyed.

Carefully, I backed the car into the garage, got out and then stood transfixed.

Through the window of the garage I had a good view of the end of the log shed and the newly-placed flagstones.

There sat the mother cat with five adorable kittens playing round her. All the unworthy thoughts of getting the R.S.P.C.A. man to capture and dispatch them humanely, vanished at once.

This was my first glimpse of the family, and I was immediately undone.

'We must never have a cat again,' did we say?

Well, we'd got six!

CHAPTER FIVE

STRATEGY

It was no light problem to be shrugged off easily. Obviously, someone must accept responsibility for the family, and equally obviously the mother cat had decided I was the one to take them all on.

Certainly, it was no use turning a blind eye to the situation. By Christmas, if we allowed nature to take her bountiful course, we should be over-run with half-starved cats in the neighbourhood.

I decided that I would stop the supply at the source. The mother cat was now very tame and affectionate, even to the point of letting me pick her up and pet her. It should be fairly simple to put her into a basket, transfer her to the vet and get her spayed.

But when?

And what about the babies? They were still suckling, although I reckoned that they must be five or six weeks old, but I knew that they could lap.

I rang up the vet and told him my six-fold troubles. After that reassuring conversation I felt my cares were halved.

'The first thing is to wean the kittens,' he told me. 'The mother's milk must dry up before we can operate. After about a fortnight bring her in.'

I doubled my order to the milkman and set to. There was a general demoting of dishes from occasional human use to daily kitten use, and a large pie-dish stood permanently filled with milk, on the flagstones.

To begin with, they would not venture forth if I were in sight, but by hiding behind a tree I was able to get a good look at the babies when they slowly emerged from the logs to lap.

There were certainly only five. One, I learned, had strayed into the road one night, from their home in the hedge, and been injured. Despite the care lavished on it all through the night by a young man in the village, it had to be dispatched the next day, as its jaw was broken and it was unable to feed.

The five that were left were fine specimens. Two were ginger and white, one a very dark tortoiseshell, one a pale clearly-marked tabby, and the biggest was black and white. The large outcast was not to be seen. Evidently, he had been successfully driven away by the mother, although he remained in the neighbourhood.

I saw him very occasionally, as dusk fell, looking round the garden for any tit-bits thrown out for the birds. But it was obvious that he had ceased to throw in his lot with Tiggy's family, and he did not linger when he saw us about.

Their appetites were prodigious. Besides milk, they cleared saucers full of minced meat, gravy, fish, and tinned food. But the largest appetite of all belonged to the mother, and I had to carry her back to the house to make sure the kittens had their chance. There was no pretty standing back or 'children first' attitude on her part. If she got there first, she ate it. It was as simple as that.

I still fed her at the house, and now that she was going to become one of the household I decided that she must have a name.

I pondered as I watched her piling into the cheapest tinned cat food obtainable, set on Tinker's old enamel plate—the same one which had held the hedgehogs' nightly bread and milk.

Well, here was my hedgehog—my Mrs Tiggywinkle. What more suitable name could there be? She should be Tig, or Tiggy. An added advantage would be that if I called 'Timmy' or 'Tinker', in moments of mental aberration, then both names were near enough to Tiggy to be accepted.

The sun continued to shine, and I lodged two wooden seed boxes on the logs so that the kittens could have somewhere to sleep and sun-bathe. Old sacks were folded and put into them for their bedding. I put two boxes ready, for I could not imagine that five such fat lumps and Tiggy could squeeze into one.

But when I approached stealthily in the mornings, I usually managed to see all six heaped up together before they caught sight of me and the five young ones fled into the interior. Tig, of course, was too interested in the dishes I carried to flee away.

I dreaded the day of Tiggy's spaying for several reasons. Should I be able to catch her? How would she stand the ten-mile journey? She had always been free. Even now, she didn't want to stay for long inside a house. How would she react to a small basket, inside a closed car?

And what about leaving her kittens? She would fight like a tiger to get back to them, I felt sure. And how would the kittens fare? Would they wander out to find her, and get

124

lost? Would rats attack them in the night if Tiggy were not there to defend them?

But it just had to be done. When the day came, Tiggy was affronted at the meagre drop of milk which was all that she was allowed for a pre-operative breakfast. She drank it resignedly, let me pick her up, and within a minute she was in the basket while I strapped the wire door shut with shaking fingers.

She seemed more bewildered than frightened, and I put her into the car with little trouble, and set off.

Then it began. The most unearthly squallings drowned the noise of the engine. When these stopped, she began a determined assault on the door, thrusting her black muzzle through a small gap at the top, and nearly giving me heart-failure at the wheel. If she managed to get her head through, the top of the door would probably snap back and trap her neck, and she would be throttled.

On the other hand, if I stopped to extricate her she might escape into the car, and I should assuredly be lacerated to the bone, at some stage or other. I made all possible speed to the surgery, uttering soothing noises which were rightly ignored by the outraged cat.

'Call back about six,' they told me at the surgery, when I handed over the baleful Tig. I felt a traitor. Mothering was Tiggy's supreme accomplishment, and I was callously robbing her of it.

On the other hand, I told myself, as I drove home to the temporary orphans, wasn't it better to have one cheerful spayed cat than one permanently pregnant one and a growing horde of unwanted kittens?

Lord knows, I thought, as I chopped up revolting raw liver in my rôle as temporary nursemaid, five were more than enough!

CHAPTER SIX

NURSEMAID TO FIVE

It was a very different Tiggy I collected at six o'clock. She lay still and quiet, in a drugged sleep, in the basket. A large, bare, grey patch showed the scar of the operation on her side.

'She'll come round in a few hours,' they assured me. 'By the way, keep her away from the kittens for a week.'

What a hope, was my private thought! However, I promised to do my best, and we returned home to put the sleeping cat in the workshop near the house. The basket door was left open, and a seed-box bed filled with fresh hay stood beside it. Milk, water and an earth tray were left for the invalid, and we went to bed and slept fitfully.

Rats the size of goats invaded the log shed, in my dreams. Occasionally, a kitten-eating snake entered too, with one or two foxes and mad dogs for good measure. It was quite a relief to get up and see for myself, when at last morning came.

There was the usual diving for cover when I arrived at the log shed, but one of the ginger and white ones remained in the seed box. She watched me put down the plates, but would not let me stroke her. Nevertheless, it was progress.

I went to the workshop to see if Tiggy were awake. She was curled up in the hay, but roused herself when I went in.

I need not have feared that my treachery would antagonise her. She was more affectionate than ever, rubbing her head against me, and as pleased as ever to see food.

She was still bemused, and after eating, fell asleep again. She slept most of that day, while I kept an anxious eye on the log shed, and put down dishes of milk and food for my charges.

In the evening, Tiggy awoke, and as I entered the workshop, she neatly dodged around my legs and escaped. I expected her to run straight to the kittens, but to my surprise she followed me to the kitchen, looking for food. This proved something which I had long suspected. Food came first with Tiggy, children second, good mother though she was.

Having eaten a hearty meal, she was returned to her sick quarters and seemed to settle down for the night. Had she forgotten the kittens, I wondered?

I viewed the possibility of acting nursemaid to five kittens, with some dismay. Nevertheless, I remembered the vet's light-hearted advice about keeping mother and kittens apart for a week. Who knows? It might be possible if things continued in this vein.

The next morning Tiggy was nowhere to be seen in the workshop. It was impossible for her to get out.

Dumbfounded, dish in hand, I surveyed the many possible hiding places. There were plenty. Stacked deckchairs, one or two old baskets, a pile of wood and two or three large cardboard boxes, all offered cover, but as I stood there, wondering where to look first, a mew came from the topmost shelf close to the ceiling. There, among the paint pots, squatted Tiggy.

To have climbed up there was a considerable feat for any cat. For Tiggy, never particularly agile and with a newly-sewn operation scar, it was a sign of her determination to escape.

I helped her down and took her into the house to feed her. As soon as the meal had gone, she made for the door. She was herself again, and had remembered the kittens.

For an hour or so, I did my best to distract her attention, but the position was hopeless. At last, I let her out—vet or no vet—and she hustled off purposefully to the log shed. I followed her, at a distance, and watched the reunion.

It was well worth seeing. Tiggy made little chirruping noises as she approached the flagstones, and out of the logs tumbled the kittens. They rubbed their heads round Tiggy and before long she had settled down in the sunshine, surrounded by the family, and began to give each one a thorough wash. Obviously, I had fallen down badly on this part of kitten care.

I returned to the house, glad to hand over some of my duties to Tiggy, but apprehensive about any accidental damage or infection of the scar.

*   *   *

I need not have worried. All the cats flourished, and now began an amusing phase of the kitten-rearing.

As soon as Tiggy heard me about, first thing in the morning, she appeared for food. Usually, I took the kittens' dish up to the flagstones whilst she fed in the kitchen. This gave them a chance to have a meal before their mother found it.

Sometimes, I was too busy cooking my own breakfast and putting down Tiggy's, to go to the log shed immediately. The kittens' meal would have to wait a while.

But this did not suit Tiggy. As soon as her

own hunger was satisfied, she hurried back to the log shed to see that the babies had been supplied. And if they had not, then back she bustled, in a very determined fashion, to let me know that I was slipping in my duties.

She mewed plaintively until I carried the food to the flagstones, and waited to see me put it down before making the particular chirruping sound which brought them forth from their hiding places. There was no doubt about it, Tiggy now looked upon me as a mother's help, and one who needed a pretty firm hand too, if the job were to be properly done.

CHAPTER SEVEN

THE WILY BROOD

And so we settled down to a rough and ready routine. Luckily, we were not going away that summer, so that the kittens had most of our attention.

The next problem was to find homes, and this meant, of course, taming them enough to accept human beings as friends.

This was a daunting task, I knew, and I was given no encouragement by well-intentioned friends, who assured me lugubriously that it was absolutely impossible to expect kittens born in such circumstances to become really domesticated.

I was inclined to believe them. Certainly, Tiggy's training was going to be difficult to undo. She ruled them with a rod of iron, and one of the first rules they had learnt was to keep away from human beings.

She kept a sharp eye on their playing places too. They were allowed to play only within a few yards of their home, but she showed them how to climb an old plum tree, close at hand, and taught them how to hunt at night. There were plenty of gruesome remains on the flagstones in the morning, and I noticed how sharply the kittens watched the birds in the hedges.

She refused to let them come near the house, looking upon it, I believe, as her own particular preserve, a place of refreshment, and a haven from the cares of motherhood.

Once or twice, we saw them following her across the lawn to the house, but each time she chased them back, cuffing them severely if they gave trouble. It did one's heart good to see such firm parental discipline!

Nevertheless, it made my own task much more difficult. How could I get these babies to trust me, and other human beings? It was no good expecting people to give homes to kittens as wild as these were. In any case, I could not hope to catch them, at this stage.

The only thing to do was to accustom them

to human society, and to win their trust with food and affection, in that order!

It was plain that the task was going to be formidable. I was the only one willing to make advances. The five kittens were resolutely anti-social and fled at my approach. An occasional paw or tail could be seen through the chinks of the logs, but these remained motionless and unresponsive.

It was a daunting outlook.

I took to spending hours sitting perched on a good stout log on the flagstones. Beside me was a plate of tempting food, such as morsels of raw liver, to help my endeavours.

It was not as arduous as it sounds. The sun streamed down very pleasantly there in the mornings, and I quite enjoyed idling my time away waiting for kittens to appear.

I kept up a flow of encouraging noises. After all, they had to get used to the human voice, and to associate it, I hoped, with food and stroking.

It was a long job. The first to succumb to blandishment was one of the little ginger and white ones. She had always been the last to flee, and always looked slightly sleepy, so that she was known as 'the dopey one'. After a week or so, she let me stroke her head as she fed.

The others were less amenable. It took over a week of patient sitting and talking before they would all venture forth. Even then, they approached the dish very warily, ready to dash back among the logs if I moved.

Gradually, I encouraged them to take morsels of meat from my hand.

All this took a great deal of time, but it was most encouraging to see them becoming tamer as the weeks passed.

One morning, Dopey looked even dopier than usual. She sat still and shivered, and I transferred her, without any struggling on her part, to another box of hay which I put in the closed end of the shed, where she would have more shelter.

It was plain that she was ill, and I put Tiggy in with her, propping open the door so that she could visit the other kittens easily.

She was very solicitous towards the little invalid, washing her gently and curling up in the hay with her for the night. I made up my mind to see the vet if the kitten were no better in the morning.

But the vet was not needed, for when I looked into the shed the next morning Dopey lay dead. Tiggy, roused from sleep, seemed quite unconcerned, and came back to the house with me for her breakfast.

Her appetite, despite this family bereavement, remained unimpaired, and poor little Dopey was buried in the shrubbery near Tinker and Timmy.

CHAPTER EIGHT

GOOD HOMES WANTED

It was now the end of September, some five or six weeks since my first glimpse of the kittens, and they were all quite big enough to leave their mother if only homes could be found for them and—even more important—if we could catch them!

Of course, I envisaged the ideal home for my charges. It should be well away from busy roads, with grass to play in and nibble and trees to climb. Then, too, for such timid kittens, it would be best if each were the only pet in the household. Preferably there should be no young children who might mishandle them through ignorance. I have seen too many kittens, gripped in over-loving hands, who, when they retaliated with a scratch, were punished unfairly.

The prospective owners I intended to see. I was not going to part with a kitten which might be passed on elsewhere to an unknown and, possibly, cruel fate.

No, it must be *a good home*, in every sense of the word, providing affection, proper care, food, space and warmth.

It would not be easy. I might be forced to compromise, but those were my standards, and

I was lucky enough, when the time came, to be able to keep to them with only minor adjustments.

I must have asked dozens of people if they would like a kitten. Either they had one already, or had promised to have one, or they had a dog which would devour a kitten on sight, or one of the family was allergic to fur, or the traffic was a hazard, or they just simply hated cats!

Heavens, how I worked! It really looked, at one stage, as if all my efforts to prepare the kittens for domesticity were doomed to failure.

The first gleam of hope came from my hairdresser who listened to my tale of anguish and said calmly:

'I'll have one for my sister. Is there a black and white one?'

There was indeed—the finest of the remaining four—and he was now ear-marked for a perfect home. Luckily too, he was now as tame as Dopey had been, and allowed us to stroke him.

Although I knew that there was a little boy of two, called Richard, in the household, I had no fears for the kitten's mishandling. He was already a cat-lover, and had been trained by his wise mother to be very gentle with animals. I felt pretty sure that these two would grow up together very happily.

One evening a week or so later, I put down a trail of liver across the flagstones to the open

135

cat basket, and the black and white kitten obligingly walked in.

He stood the journey equably, and was introduced into his new home. I thought about him often that night, and hoped he would settle down away from his mother and the rest of the family. How would he like being in a house, I wondered, after being so free?

I was told the next day that this mite from the backwoods spent his first evening sitting on the couch in his new home, watching television.

George—for that was to be his name—was obviously an adaptable cat.

I have weekly bulletins on his progress. He has an enormous appetite, and obviously takes after his mother in this respect. He takes a keen interest in Richard's model cars, and in the cat next door, called William, whose food he eats as well as his own. George certainly fell on his feet.

Another cat-loving friend came to the rescue. He put up a notice in the local bank where he works, and through this kind effort two more homes were found.

Two newly-married young girls came to inspect the kittens one evening. There were now only three to choose from: the ginger and white one, the dark tortoiseshell, called Smokey, and the light stripey one.

We stood, strategically placed behind a hedge, to watch them feed. The prospective owners were delighted with the sight, and made their choice.

'If I can catch the right one,' I was obliged to stipulate. 'Or any of them, for that matter!'

Both were happy to co-operate. If I could not catch the right kitten for each, then whichever was delivered would be welcome, they assured me. As for sex, they were quite happy to let the vet sort out that little matter when the time came.

They could not have been kinder, and I was greatly relieved. Good homes ... really good homes ... for three!

'There's just one thing,' said one of the girls as we returned to the house. 'A stray cat comes to my house and I feed it. I hope it will get on with this new kitten.'

We easily brushed aside the visiting stray, in our present care-free mood, and promised to deliver the kittens in about three weeks' time.

I soon realised that I should have taken that stray cat more seriously. After all, I had plenty of experience with strays by this time.

A few days later, the girl telephoned in some distress.

'That cat,' she said distractedly, 'has just moved in *with a kitten*! I shall simply have to adopt them. Can you find another home for yours?'

I knew exactly how she felt. So recently had I suffered the same dismay and helplessness. I assured her that my kitten would either stay here or be found a home, and we parted with mutual sympathy.

But I was particularly sorry about this set-back, for this kitten's home would have been ideal . . . a cottage set well back from the road, in commonland thick with bracken . . . a cat's idea of heaven! But it was not to be.

* * *

It was comparatively easy to catch the remaining ginger and white kitten and to transport her to her new home, which was a modern house on a new estate. She would be the only pet. There was a garden, and plenty of open grassy places in front of the houses. The new owner was used to cats and a true cat-lover, and I felt sure that this kitten would be very lucky.

But her release in the new home was anything but tranquil. She horrified us all by dashing wildly about the room, until at last, exhausted, she took refuge behind a curtain.

I was extremely worried about this kitten, but was relieved to hear from another friend that she gradually settled down.

And so we were left with two kittens. One was the tabby, which we called 'the stripey one', and the other the dark tortoiseshell known as 'Smokey'. Both were decidedly frisky, and tore away into the neighbours' gardens whenever we approached.

Stripey was a particular favourite of mine—beautifully marked, with here and there a touch of ginger among the clear tabby stripes. A home awaited him in a quiet road in the local market town.

'He's still quite wild,' I told the couple anxiously.

They were unperturbed.

'Our last cat was completely crazy,' they told me comfortingly, and obviously it had flourished happily with them for many years. It was plain that Stripey would be going to an understanding home.

We arranged a day for his delivery. I was confident that this one was male, although I had told the prospective owners cautiously that I did not know to which sex Stripey belonged, and they were game to take the chance.

He really was adorable. I sometimes came upon him washing his small face, or climbing the old plum tree with Smokey, who was by far the most adventurous climber of the family.

The two were inseparable. Smokey was wilder than Stripey, if anything, and now that the two were so much together they seemed to grow more independent, and wary of my overtures.

On the evening of Stripey's move, I repeated my usual strategy of a liver trail, but Stripey would have none of it. I think, looking back, that he saw us put one of the other kittens into the basket and carry it to the car. He wasn't going to have anything to do with that contraption!

The next morning we went apologetically to the house and confessed that we had been beaten. We would try again.

We tried many times during the next two weeks, and always the result was the same. Stripey and Smokey took one look at us as we approached, and dashed away across the gardens to cover.

We were utterly defeated.

Sadly, full of apologies, we had to tell the prospective owners that it was hopeless, and that some tamer, luckier kitten must be sought for by them. They were very understanding, and I only hope that they finally found a more amenable cat.

It looked now as though we must face having three cats on the establishment. Tiggy had now settled in well, sitting on our laps, curling up on the sunniest bed, and generally behaving as though she had lived with us for years.

She revelled in the warmth and comfort of a house, and showed her appreciation with a display of affection which was touching.

The weather was now becoming chilly. The leaves were tumbling down from the trees, and the first frosts arrived.

The logs were beginning to be used, and we put a cat-flap on the workshop door, nearer the house. This was a strong weatherproof building which would provide warmth and shelter for the two half-grown cats who were still too scared to come indoors.

I took to putting their food and drink in there, and provided two seed-box beds stuffed with hay.

They quickly learned to push up the cat-flap, and each morning there were hollows in the hay beds where they had slept.

This state of affairs continued for several weeks, and then one morning a tragedy occurred.

Smokey's body was found on the grass verge outside the cottage. She had obviously been run down by a vehicle and from the nature of the injuries, she must have died instantly.

Stripey definitely missed his companion during the next few days and wandered about, mewing pitifully. He took to running to Tiggy whenever she appeared, and although she was kind, in an off-hand way, she did not encourage him to come indoors.

Now that he was bereft and the weather was becoming so cold, I decided to let Stripey share the house with his mother. It was pretty plain, by this time, that we were destined to keep Stripey as well as Tiggy, and certainly we were so attached to him that we could not have parted from him easily after all our vicissitudes together.

He took to coming into the kitchen for his

food, and now that Smokey had gone, he seemed readier to accept human companionship. Naturally, the cold weather helped our efforts, and very soon he ate regularly indoors, and found that the hearthrug in front of the stove was the perfect place for comfort.

Tiggy resented his presence strongly. She growled whenever he came in, and did her best to drive him away. It says much for Stripey's spirit that he bravely resisted her attacks, but he had to put up with many a cuff and spit.

It took some weeks before Tiggy accepted the inevitable and let him settle in on equal terms. Even now she chooses the best spot in the room, and Stripey has to make do with what is left.

Tiggy is quite aware that she is the top cat, and we are only too ready to accept the situation. After all, she has worked hard enough for her position.

CHAPTER NINE

THE TWO WHO STAYED

Stripey was now six months old and the right age to be neutered.

It was comparatively easy to catch him now that he was indoors, and we set out with a yowling basket of furious cat, one January day.

'Male or female?' the girl had asked me when I rang up to make an appointment.

'No idea,' I told her cheerfully.

We delivered Stripey to the vet's care and went home to prepare the workshop as a temporary convalescent home again.

'One thing,' we told each other, 'it's a much simpler operation for a male.'

We thought again.

'If Stripey is a male,' we added.

As we might have guessed, Stripey was a female, despite her boyish looks and behaviour. She spent two days as a pampered patient and then romped back to normality, only the scar showing any sign of invalidism.

An interesting thing was that her fur took almost twice as long as Tiggy's to grow thick enough to cover the scar. Certainly, her fur is softer and finer than her mother's, but Tiggy was operated on in September when her winter coat was about to grow. This may have been one reason for the difference in time.

Incidentally, it was on the occasion of Stripey's first outing after her operation, as she was pottering vaguely about the lawn, that I saw the large brindled tom cat for the last time. Bolder than he had ever been, he appeared at dusk and made amorous advances to the somewhat surprised Stripey.

He rolled about seductively, giving strident love-sick cries. Fearful of any harm to Stripey's new scar, we chased her suitor away, and brought the lady indoors.

'Just in time!' was my first thought, congratulating myself on having the operation safely over. But I heard later that this is quite a common occurrence. A newly-spayed female attracts the male just as if she were on heat.

What became of the tom-cat, whom we thought of as the outcast, we do not know. He was a splendid animal, magnificently strong, and he may have moved away to another territory where he could be king. Or he may have met a sad end on this dangerous stretch of road, as so many more have done.

But there is yet another development. Recently, a small brindled female cat, so strange-looking with her large pointed ears and sharp muzzle that she has been nicknamed 'Foxy' by my neighbour, has appeared and produced four fine kittens. She too has been befriended by the two kind-hearted maids. Could this be the big outcast kitten who tried so hard to join Tiggy's younger ones, and is now repeating family history? We shall never know.

*   *   *

Tiggy and Stripey have now settled down together very affectionately. If anything, Tiggy is the more playful, starting the evening fight which they both enjoy. They greet each other with much head-rubbing and mutual washing when they meet, and have even become so accommodating as to share one plate of food.

We little realised how fond we should become of Tiggy and her family. That first shock of dismay when we found that we were to be their unwilling hosts, fast changed to admiration and devotion.

We have learnt a lot in these last few months, which is why I thought it worthwhile to record these true events. For one thing, it seems that kittens, however wild, do respond to companionship—with the help of food, of course.

The response varies, naturally. I feel quite sure that Smokey would never have become as tame as Tiggy is now. I doubt if Stripey will ever be quite as relaxed and demonstrative as her mother, but she is nevertheless, a charming household pet. I think we have proved that it is possible to tame such young wild ones, despite the gloomy prognostications of our friends who, I think, doubted our sanity when coming upon us at our lonely vigils by the logs.

But we have learned most of all from Tiggy herself. One cannot help marvelling at the courage and ingenuity of that starving little mother cat who set out to overcome all the obstacles in her path to provide for her family, and triumphed superbly.

Her success has brought great happiness to

us all, and it is to Tiggy that we make our final salute.

We hope you have enjoyed this Large Print book. Other Chivers Press or Thorndike Press Large Print books are available at your library or directly from the publishers.

For more information about current and forthcoming titles, please call or write, without obligation, to:

Chivers Press Limited
Windsor Bridge Road
Bath BA2 3AX
England
Tel. (01225) 335336

OR

Thorndike Press
P.O. Box 159
Thorndike, Maine 04986
USA
Tel. (800) 223-2336

All our Large Print titles are designed for easy reading, and all our books are made to last.